Sitting on the Prime Minister's Right Hand

Sitting on the Prime Minister's Right Hand

Political and Social Commentary
by Sir Bruce Fernargle-Jones

With Selected Items from the Archive of
the Rottnest Island Film Commission

BILL LYON

FOREWORD BY ROY CLEGHORN

EDITED BY NEIL RATTIGAN

2019

Fastnet Books
227 Donnelly Street
Armidale, New South Wales, 2350
Australia

www.fastnetbooks.net
publishing@fastnetbooks.net
buvelot@optusnet.com.au

First published 2019

National Library of Australia
Cataloguing-in-Publication entry:

Lyon, William John – 1956-2019
Sitting on the Prime Minister's Right Hand

ISBN-13: 978-0-9874587-4-2
ISBN-10: 0-9874587-4-4

For Robert Broadfield

FOREWORD

ROY CLEGHORN
Noted bush walker and camper
Author of Roy's Big Book of Bush Bities

I first met Sir Bruce Fernargle-Jones (or plain Brucie Jones as he then was) at the time that I was not only Australia's foremost television naturalist but also an undercover ASIO agent tasked with keeping a close eye on clandestine outback activities. Sir Bruce (as he was to become) was wandering the Outback in an endeavour to avoid Doris Ghumboyle, who, since she tracked him down, he later married and who became in time Lady Fernagle-Jones. (Doris, that is, not Bruce.)

Two weeks of taking tight hold of my tripod and firmly placing it where I insisted it should go provided Sir Bruce (as he was to become) with the necessary skills and insights into the visual media industry to enable him to be offered and to accept the position of Chairman of the newly created Rottnest Island Film Commission. (Film Commissions were all the rage at the time and were being set up everywhere and anywhere.) Recognising the debt for the valuable opportunities he had gained by living, breathing, eating and working in such close proximity to and with me, Sir Bruce (as he necessarily became on appointment to the RIFC) asked me to 'join the board'. Offering the merry quip that I had no skills as a carpenter, I nonetheless accepted with alacrity the position and the remuneration.

Although a senate inquiry or two in subsequent years led to the disbanding of the RIFC, I am proud to say that, working in harness with Sir Bruce, we were able to make valuable creative inputs into several unsung and unproduced classics of the Australian Cinema, namely *Gone With the Wobbegong*, *A Bandicoot Too Far* and *A Quokka Lips Now*.*

Sir Bruce, no slouch in the race towards new technology, discovered radio about the same time as radio discovered him. A barely known radio network with the alphabetically uninspired name of the ABC noted Sir Bruce's burgeoning pre-eminence as an astute observer of Australian culture, society and politics, and reputation as a crashing bore and insisted that he enhance the airwaves with his considered views on the state of the nation. Needing to get out of the house and away from Lady Fernagle-Jones he condescended to allow his dulcet tones to grace the ABC's schedules on an occasional basis. His incisive and insightful commentaries on the contemporary and vital issues of the hour, day, week, month, etc. no doubt contributed to fundamental changes in the Australian *zeitgeist* (whatever that is). Those wise enough to purchase and read this precious collection of Sir Bruce's broadcasts will have little option but to concur (although they may well be required to clean it up if they do).

Since being forced off the air by combination of those in the ABC jealous of his broadcasting ability and those in the political and cultural maelstrom whose egos were regularly punctured by his devastating critiques, Sir Bruce has done bugger-all. But he has done it with his inevitable *sang-froid* (whatever that is) and with both eyes to the main chance.

Bide-a-Wee Aged Care and Asbestos Processing Facility,
Widgiemooltha
2000

* See Neil Rattigan, *Images of Australia: 100 Films of the New Australia Cinema* (1991) in which the author totally ignores these films, carrying 'unsung' to new depths and revealing what a clot the author is – editor.

Editorial Comment

Sadly, it must be reported that Sir Bruce Fernargle-Jones moved on to the Great Brown-nosing Land in the Sky in 2019.

Previously, the last that had been known of Roy was when he was seen heading out into the Simpson Desert, claiming to be scouting locations for a planned Rottnest Island Film Commission production, The Wombat That Ate Ayres Rock. *He had been neither seen nor heard from since until the St Vincent De Paul organisation tracked him in order to return a heap of stained Bombay Bloomers and used khaki singlets he had dumped at their Op Shop in Birdsville in 1985.*

PART I

THUS SPAKE SIR BRUCE

The items that are found in the following pages are transcripts of 'talks' given by Bill Lyon* in the persona of Sir Bruce Fernargle-Jones on ABC[§] radio between 1989 and 1993. (Details of the origins of Sir Bruce Fernargle-Jones and the Rottnest Island Film Commission, to which he often referred, are given in Part II.) The voice of Sir Bruce was, thus, that of Bill Lyon – with a touch of E.G. Whitlam[†].

The broadcasts were made live late at night in a programme presented by Robert Broadfield. Although they originated in the Perth studio of the ABC they were heard nationwide. Some evidence exists, in the form of 'feedback' fax from listeners, that the programme and therefore Sir Bruce were heard in a variety of different places from northern Queensland to Tasmania and across Australia from East to West. And, it may be inferred, that Sir Bruce had something of a following– among 'night owls' as the programme was broadcast late at night.

The actual date of each 'talk' is not precisely known as no dates are recorded on the hand-written scripts from which pages have been transcribed and, as far as is known, the ABC made no attempt to record and archive them.

Several decades later the thought occurred to Lyon that there might be some value in collecting the scripts of the talks together with a view to publication. It was felt that this was task that could be undertaken after Lyon retired; he was a full-time secondary school teacher in his working life. Regretfully, the Grim Reaper knocked on his door and demanded admission before the task could be undertaken.

What follows, therefore, are transcriptions from a large number of hand-written 'scripts'. The use of inverted commas around 'scripts' is intended to refer to the fact that the material was intended to be both read and spoken (or performed, really) by Lyon and, as 'straightman', Robert Broadfield. Because he also wrote them all, there were opportunities for improvisation by Lyon, further assisted by Broadfield. In short, the existing material was not written by Lyon in perfect prose. And, as noted, the broadcasts were not recorded (this was pre-digital and analogue recording required bulky magnetic tape) and so the transcriptions that follow are, at best, reconstructions from hand-written originals. These reconstructions do not, of course, take into account the interchanges between Lyon and Broadfield nor of improvised gags, jokes or comments.

Even so, there has been no attempt to modify or emend the scripts beyond the necessity on occasion to insert a word, term or phrase that may be absent but which can be inferred from the text or the context. These insertions are rendered within square brackets. Here and there, it has been felt necessary to resort to the editorial [sic] meaning that a word or term is as it was written even if, to the editor, it seemed wrong. And once or twice, the editor was simply puzzled by what was meant and thus was driven to insert a [?].

Even allowing for inexorable rise of 'political correctness' in the decades since this material went before a microphone, no attempt has been made 'soften' or censure the occasional moments when today's alleged more delicate sensitivities might be (or might be claimed to be) bruised.

These transcriptions, then, will have to serve the historical purposes of records (mayhap flawed) of Sir Bruce in full flight. The humour, quips, the insights and barbed stings are all Bill Lyon's.

---

* *William John Lyon, 1956-2019.*

§ *For any readers who may have the ill-fortune to dwell outside Australia, ABC is the acronym of the Australian Broadcasting Commission, Australia's national public radio and television network.*

† *Gough Whitlam was Leader of the Australian Labor Party from 1967 to 1977, and Prime Minister from 1972 to 1975. He had a particular way of speaking which lent itself to imitation.*

IT'S NOT ONLY on Bob Hawke's right hand that I've sat but I am prepared to reveal that I've also rested on the digital protuberances of a number of US presidents.

It was Sir Bruce Fernargle-Jones that said that immortal, prophetic comment in Dallas: 'Go ahead, Jack, leave the top down, it's a bonza day!'

Well, luckily Lady Fernargle-Jones made up for that gaff. She has a handy hint for removing stains from pink nylon.

I lent a hand to the Ford presidency. To some people, standing up isn't as easy as it looks. By the end of his presidency Gerry remembered that the important thing about standing up is trying to remember not to fall over.

It's not only on a domestic level that the Fernargle-Jones influence, the firm guiding hand, is felt.

I was there backing up Dick Nixon in China. Actually, behind and to the side.

The reason such a staunch anti-communist wound up in China was that I booked Dick on Japan Airlines as Air Force One was having its engines counted by the Central Intelligence Agency, so it was out of action for few months.

I digress. Japan Airlines have combat experienced pilots. They're very good, but they like to turn up unannounced and unexpected, arriving out of the sun.

Anyway, the trip was a big diplomatic success. Chou En-Lai taught me everything I know about non-starch washing and Dick picked up Mao's recipe for sweet-and-sour pork.

I don't hold with all this talk about Dick's presidency. He had all the qualifications: he was a car dealer, he was American, husband to Pat and Daddy to Tricia.

Of course, Ron as President took on board the collective Fernargle-Jones wisdom and that's quite an intellectual leap for a man with the brain of a chook.

I was there for the disarmament talks in Reykjavik, just us three mates together.

Mike Gorbachev conceded a few missiles he was prepared to dismantle and provided a comprehensive five-year plan for doing it.

Ron wasn't prepared to concede anything. He wasn't aware what disarmament was, thought Star Wars was great movie (especially the cute, furry Ewoks) and had a fair sort of idea that Mike was of Russian extraction.

THERE IS A disturbing amount of criticism about to be levelled at the Labor Party.

It's unfair, and it's not very well-informed.

Not enough has been said in recent days about what Bob and the boys – the government – have been doing in their stewardship of this wide-brown-thing.

What's Bob thinking, where's government going or where the party thinks Bob is going, or where the party think it's going, or where Bob's thinking has gone, or where the party's thinking has gone and who saw it last – probably Peter Abels.

Bob, the Prime Minister, has made an extensive, fully carpeted fool out of himself with this bagging [of] Paul Keating of [?] succession to the dynastic crown.

You don't see the Liberals making fools out of themselves, costing the country air-fares and businesses lunches.

They've been more sensible and put a revolving door in the office of the Leader of the Opposition.

And what are the Liberals doing at this point of time?

They've taken my advice, taking the opportunity to capitalise by tearing themselves apart in New South Wales.

That'll rattle Bob!

Just about the thing to hog the headlines for days when Hewson and his crowd want to be seen as resolute and united – what achievers – they *still* want a consumption tax.

I don't understand what they've got against weak, sickly, coughing children.

Well, now that Bob's got John 'the Jelly-fish' Kiernan in charge of the economy...

And Simon 'I've been head of the ACTU so I can be P.M. one day too' Crean in charge of the next rural crisis.

Paul's waiting for Christie's next catalogue and that arrives in six-month's time.

IT'S BEEN BILLED as the biggest tussle since Harold Holt and the monster squid of Port Phillip Bay.

I'd like to have a word or two about where Paul Keating and I stand, with relation, assumed by either one of us, or the stance assumed by anybody else, with regard to the leadership.

And Robert, we're invited in this!

Of course, sitting as I do on Bob's left hand or is it right, it's natural for Paul and I to be seen putting our heads together in an intimate way – for a discreet chinwag about the way things are going.

There's a body of opinion, particularly from the fourth estate, that Bob and Paul communicate only through their seconds. This tapestry of lies could split the party asunder. We're not going to fall for it.

Bob is a wonderful leader.

He's a man of [*sic*] immersed in the parliamentary experience. He's one of the few left from the Whitlam era.

The staggering political acumen that gave us the wages breakout of 1974 has been, once again, harnessed to produce this recession we had to have.

Paul wants people to know it wasn't all his doing.

After all, this is a democracy and what people want is entirely academic.

And remember Paul is a man of accomplishment; he's made a remarkable achievement in economics.

And there can be little doubt that I support Bob Hawke.

THIS IS AN opportune moment to have a look at the festive season - a traditional event very much with us [just] when we wish it wasn't.

I've noticed that many people tend to forget the significance of Christmas. For those people Christmas starts with an office party and ends [when] you've realised what you've spent. Christmas has replaced Lent as a period of penance.

You knock over your twenty-nine course Christmas dinner that some aged relative has whipped up on a forty-six-degree day and promptly melted into the lino in the process. You sat there as adult member of the family reel and convulse with the spirit of the occasion.

All the time the sprogs and the ankle-biters are rubbing pre-masticated chocolate into the draperies.

Of course you can't be too concerned with the flippant things.

You ignore the pack and nasty and useless aspects of your family and how truly depleted the gene stock must be.

You put aside personal discomfort as you witness the remarkable breakdown of taste and intelligence as the gifts are handed out.

But think of those that have selflessly gone out of their way to make this Christmas special.

The retailers – toting up sale after sale on those cash registers.

Television and musical entertainers who leave their loved ones in August to record a television special of reggae Christmas carols.

All so we – you and I – can enjoy our Chrissy dinny, opening our pressies with the relies in our jammies in front of the telly.

A LOT OF people wrote and called about the bucketing that we gave Senator Graham Richardson last week on the programme.

When I say a lot of people, I mean Richo called and wrote a note pasted together out of the news type telling me to tone it down or he'd hand my wife over to the New South Wales right.

Richo's a clever political operator – unlike many, say Richo's best, sorry, former best mate and leader Hawkie – Richo was able to get his resignation sent off before the acceptance came in.

Being a member of parliament is by no means all beer and skittles.

As we've pointed out in this programme only last week, it's obvious that men like Richo, Beazley and Ray have played the skittle element down to the bare minimum.

Richo said to me, as he ate a cow in parliamentary dining room, that politics is full of intrigue. 'People are never as they seem, Sir Bruce.'

And if Richo tells you this you have to appreciate it.

'Politics has lost a good deal of its dignity,' Richo went on to say, and he ought to know, he eliminated most of it. How else could you have such a delightful cross-factional brawl over Richo's deckchair?

Richo leaves the cabinet on the highest note with Paul [...]

After all, Richo was instrumental in Paul's attempt on the pole vault record.

Richo's last bit of advice before the forty-four gallons of ice-cream arrived for dessert was politics can be a rewarding career but remember to cut blazes in trees, so you can come back again, and keep the pocket knife sharpened just in case the native bearers on the left turn out to have another agenda.

1991: A YEAR where commie, pinko muck-rakers such as yourself Gerry had to sober-up and race to keep up with events.

There was young – well, youngish – and handsome in a Bob Hoskins sort of way, Mike Gorbachev being rolled by the charismatic – well, charismatic by the old, fat Politburo standards – Boris Yeltson.

1991 also saw that bastard at the family reunion of nations South Africa have trade sanctions and cultural embargoes lifted. This means we will have to listen to them at the UN in their language that sounds like a cartoon character.

In Australia, it was a tough time for old mates. Sir Terry Lewis was convicted of receiving a few grand from colourful identities. Which means if organised crime can afford to do that, how little must they spend on office supplies?

Another old mate, the balding, charismatic ex-premier of Western Australia, Brian Burke, demonstrated how someone with leadership potential and an interest in diplomacy needs a hobby and a secretary with amnesia.

In the media, my advice was ignored with regard to what to do with the ABC: get Westpac to throw a heap of folding stuff at it, lose the lot and change its name to Channel Ten.

Financially, in 1991, saw my advice hold true: buy things of value – Filipino brides, Korean babies and Queensland politicians.

Most importantly, Paul Keating now leads the party that made the man most people thought should have been the prime minister in this time of crisis the governor-general.

CHRISTMAS AT THE LODGE.

It was billed as the biggest tussle since Harold Holt took on monster squid in Port Phillip Bay.

Well, what can I say about our new prime minister that isn't constantly said by members of the BLF and the wharfies?

Paul Keating is a man who makes Bill Hayden look less than ordinary.

Sitting, as I do, on Paul's right hand, it's natural for Paul and I to be seen putting our heads together in an intimate way for a discreet chinwag.

Of course, Paul doesn't have the staggering political acumen of Bob Hawke – the man who gave us the wages breakout of the '70s and the only cut in 'real' wages during a period of enormous corporate profit.

Paul has only given us 'the recession we had to have'.

And Paul wants people to know that it wasn't all his doing.

After all, the Parliamentary Labor Party is a democracy and what the back-benchers want is entirely academic.

Paul is a man of pregnant [sic] accomplishment or -ments, given the popularity of the Compass Appeal around the nation, raising 4.5 million dollars to save the St Vincent De Paul of the Air.

Paul and I are going to launch a series of fund-raisers for our recently impoverished entrepreneurs: the Alan Bond Lamington Drive; the 'Bob-a-Job' Laurie Connell Chook Raffle; the Chris Skase telethon because of medical costs.

SIR BRUCE AS ADVISER TO BRIAN BURKE.

The vexed business of making investments personal, professional and for one's leader's fund and/or political party.

This is a wonderful leisure activity for balding, charismatic types with leadership potential or diplomacy [potential?].

Some people get so carried away they hire friends, relatives and office space and do it all [in] the term of their office. It's a dangerous attitude – it's best to treat the whole thing as nothing more than a hobby for the balding, etc.

Have a bit of fun but don't take it seriously – invest in art or stamps, or antiques and stamps, or soccer clubs or stamps.

You will need another broker – they're easy to find because they wear stockings over their heads and have a black eye-patch.

Having done this, just buy a few [stamps] until you get the feel of it.

Then keep an eye out (preferably the one without the patch) for someone to trade or sell to.

If you make a profit, then that's very wonderful and all that goes into the leader's fund. But don't try and do it every time or you'll lose the thrill of the chase.

Sometimes, stamp collecting for the balding, charismatic types with leadership potential or diplomacy [potential] can cause acute embarrassment.

Staff forget whose stamps are whose, everyone gets fired, the gut [sic] doesn't flip the coin the same way and the turf's had a bit too much rain or there was no supplementary number to speak of.

There you go, and if you lose a few hundred thousand, you can't be surprised – good hobbies if you're the balding, etc type, and, like amnesiac private secretaries, they are hard to find. But not as hard as the Party's stamps among your own.

13

PRINCE CHARLES – 'Chassa' to his close friends of course, 'Chucka Windsor' to his Hooray Henry pals down at the severely privileged polo club – has had his remarks about education widely reported.

Charles is opposed to progressive methods of teaching – they're just fashionable trends. He favours more formal teaching methods.

He clearly remembered being hit over the head with a polo mallet by his father (the Duke) when Phil was attempting to teach Chassa how to make a double-meat souvlaki to go.

Chassa is absolutely correct that we do not know how much or which Shakespeare is being taught.

His Royal Highness remarked to me that he had fond memories of Geelong or Timbertop that were very fond. And he remembered Geelong quite clearly and Timbertop well, because and without a moment's hesitation he added that he had gone to school there for a period...

Shakespeare anyway was the topic, wasn't it? Anyway Chuck appreciated learning Shakespeare, the barge of Avalon, through process rather than content stressed lessons.

As Chassa says, everything he knows about 'A Midsummer Prince of Hamet', he learnt while being concussed with a Sovereign Don Bradman School Boy's cricket bat.

Chuck pointed out to me that many parents that he knew – people with more money than God, titles, stately houses *and* on the Civil List – shared low expectations of their children.

That's why they packed them off to boarding school and got a dog, something they could love.

And we can see Chassa and his lovely wife Eccles... And they do get on. Absolutely. Very well. They speak to each other quite often, and even to the children.

Anyway, I digress. They have put their kiddies into the Prince's education firing line – putting the royal ankle-biters where Chassa's mouth is.

And didn't Prince Billy do well on his first effort? I bet this next King of England, Scotland, Ireland (North), Wales and Australia remembers his three-times table now that he has had a Slazenger 2 wood wrapped around his royal little bonce.

He's going to be just like his dad.

I WAS ACTUALLY held against my will in the Lebanon.

Now, as an experienced traveller, I packed with just such an event [in mind], extra shirts, socks, surgical support, rocket-propelled grenades and flak jacket.

I was there in my function as part-time trouble shooter for the United Nations and scouting locations for the Rottnest Island Film Commission's next production *The Dirty Dozen's Harum Holiday*.

The radical Hezbollah grabbed me as I was making my way through the tastefully bullet-riddled grandeur that was nice Beirut.

I was bundled into a Renault. Renaults are the favoured vehicles for kidnapping and car bombs. So avoid double-parked *le cars* – if you catch my drift.

Apart from waving a semi-automatic weapon in my face and chatting at the top of their lungs, not much happened.

Not all these people were stern zealots. Some have string bikinis.

After driving at top speed, much of it on the footpaths, they got me to their little hide-away or burned out shell, as you would call it, where they serve splendid native dishes.

When danger waits the tables and death is going to carry your luggage, it adds zest to life.

They're a good natured bunch of fanatics. One of them said they'd like to do something with my mother – my Arabic is not what it should be. I suggested he might like to try whatever it was with Bob Hawke. He pointed a gun in my face and we had a good laugh.

After a few hours of me regaling my captors with tales of the massive tax advantages open to Australians under the old 10B(a) rules, they blind-folded me, spun me around three times, and I found myself in a shop that was a Pentagon parts supplier and floppy, greasy, ill-made rug vendor. Just like the ones you see advertised on television here.

John McCarthy and I had notes pinned to us so if a policeman found us, he could direct us to the UN Secretary Perez de Cuellar.

Well, as I said my Arabic's never been good, so I tore the note off and threw it away and got a cab back to the pile of rubble that was once my hotel.

HELLO, MISS JULIE here. Presenting tonight my guide to terrorist situations and distribution.

'Bass boat', 'Passbot' and 'pisspot' are the only English words that every terrorist understands and that none of the poor confused darlings can say. I think they are euphemisms for passport!

For the newcomer to terrorism, it's an endless series of faces, gun barrels (preferably non-smoking) and mispronouncing your travel documents,

But seriously though – some of the faces belong to Christian Phalange, Red Brigade, some to angry Shiites or blustering Black September or grumpy Palestinians. And who knows what the rest belong to!

But seriously though – if you're going to a terrorist destination, you'd be crazy not to have a gun.

I assure you, all the crazy people you're about to meet have guns too – isn't that nice?

If you've handed over the wrong credentials, you'll soon notice that your captors have all the paint worn off the ends of their gun barrels. Don't be hasty to judge. It's not bad terrorist housekeeping; it's rubbing against people's nose that causes that.

But seriously though – it's amazing how small the hole is where the bullet comes out but what a big difference it could make to your social schedule.

The big advantage about terrorist situations and destinations is that they are free of tour groups and Nikon-toting Japanese.

Beaches, though, are not crowded and what could be more authentic than highly cultured people armed to the teeth and bent on murder, pillage and rape?

But seriously though – just think of the slide night when or if you get back.

BASTARD AT THE family of nations' picnic.

An opportunity to talk about South Africa's return to the family of nations [via the] lifting of trade and cultural embargoes.

Let's face it, they've had a big effect on the distribution of wealth in South Africa. It's just like the United States now.

All the people who live in the really nice suburbs are white and all the people who work there – who cook, sweep and clean the driveways with their tongues – are not white. The only difference is the lady who comes around with the laundry doesn't carry it on her head in Beverley Hills or Manhattan.

Everywhere you go in the world somebody's raping women, enslaving primitive tribes-people, killing minorities in jails, setting fire to people, hunting people with automatic weapons from helicopters. The problem with South Africa is they do it all in one country and they admit it.

Rejoining the family of nations means that we'll have to listen to the South Africans at the United Nations, and their language sounds like cartoon characters. For example: 'I porked the cor in the cor pork.'

At the Rottnest Island Film Commission we've had to re-write a lot of productions now the bigoted, knuckle-headed Boers and their dumpy, white ankle-socked wives in flower-printed sun dresses cannot be used as international bad guys. I guess we'll have to use the Nazis again.

Productions the Rottnest Island Film Commission intends to flood the South African cinemas with are: the Winnie Mandela soccer team doco, *Offside with the Necklace of Death*, starring Chuck Norris as Winnie Mandela and *The Satchel of Plenty*, starring David Parker as Chief Butolasese.

THE TRIAL AND subsequent conviction of Sir Terrence Lewis has blown the gaff on the existence of organised crime in Australia.

Now we know if organised crime can slip Terry Lewis a few hundred grand, they must be making a lot of money.

Especially when one considers how little they spend on office supplies.

In the Griffith area alone they laid out no more than four thousand dollars in the last few years for stationary, and that includes Don Mackay's concrete sneakers.

Furthermore, they only have one secretary who does all the typing, and she shares her office with the Queensland Police Force Dance Studio.

Organised crime is responsible for many murders and other activities such as gambling, narcotics, prostitution and stamp collecting Western Australia.

Tentacles of the corrupt empire reach even into government. A few months ago, the Federal Police had two mafia figures under arrest. They spent the night at the Lodge, and Bob Hawke slept on the lounge.

My inquiry into organised crime suggests that it's a blight on this wide brown thing of ours.

Many young Australians could be lured into a career of crime by the promises of easy money and stamps, not realising – and here I'd like to speak directly to the young people, in and out of uniform, listening. You've got to realise that criminals work long hours, frequently in buildings without air conditioning.

Parents – what are the early tell-tale signs you kids are getting involved in organised crime?

One: they're promoted over the heads of others to a senior position in the Queensland police force.

Two: They own one of Australia's internal airlines.

Three: They fail to stop eating when a person sitting next to them is hit by a falling anvil.

Four: They habitually wear large, chunky gold jewellery and have a blanket over their heads.

Five: They have a controlling interest in an Australian media network.

EVEN IN THESE troubled times, even my mates in the corporate banking sector feel responsible to and for people.

They've adopted an open dialogue with a frank exchange of ideas between Treasury, the Government and the people.

As you know, the banking sector has come in for some pretty severe criticism for the amounts of money they have been making.

It's been said that they are excessive – but not by me.

Let's face it! They've been making this kind of profit for so long and openly that there's nothing excessive about it.

You can't expect poor people to get the gist of this.

Nobby Clarke once reached a point where he'd be embarrassed about how filthily well he'd been doing.

Bank profit levels are dictated by how much people want what the banks have a lot of...

Which is, in a nutshell, other people's money, and I think people have accepted this.

The banks give you, say, seven percent to/for the pleasure of playing the market with your money. They charge you for [them] playing with your money while they're looking after it. Then they spend your money advertising their ability to give you money you don't have but which they do, through credit cards – whereby they can charge you in excess of three times what they'd give you if you'd just spent your own money instead of theirs, ours.

Of course, bank credit card profits are illusory.

They can't even get them to pay because of the breath-taking cost of administration.

Which, in other words, it would be like you not having a wage if there's something you'd like to buy with it.

MY EXCITEMENT [IS] at being there, my personal self, intimately present at the actual moment of eventhood.

There's going to be me and seven thousand commie, pinko, muck-rakers covering this combined summit conference, missile kiss-off and Soviet-American love-in.

Soviet bureaucratic expediency being what it is, you only had to sign up eleven years in advance to get an invitation to the kick-off.

Now to many, a summit conference might be as interesting as a second cousin's wedding. Some stuff does go on that we'd like a peek at, but *that* happens behind closed doors. What we get to see is the bride and groom walking down the aisle.

But there's Gorbachev. He's young – well, youngish, and handsome in a Bob Hoskins sort of way, and highly charismatic by the old, fat Politburo Central Committee standards. And he's got a wife, Raisa, who everyone agrees is very life-like. And who doesn't look like she rolled off the tank assembly line in Minsk in 1943.

George Bush's right-wing ex-pals must be wondering.

They want to know: Is the Gipper channelling?

They assumed that George was a conservative Republican, at least in this incarnation.

What happened to the die-hard Bolshie-hater who couldn't stand dumpy bald guys who hardly spoke English?

George really likes 'Splotch Top' – that is his nickname for Mike.

They're united in their hatred for liberals.

George thinks they should be deported to Russia and 'Spot' Gorbachev believes they should be sent to Siberia.

Of course, liberals think good super-power relations will put a stop to another Hitler or Mussolini. Tell that to Saddam Hussein!

IT'S BEEN FOURTEEN years since Elvis Presley joined up as first mate on Harold Holt's submarine affaire.

When I first ran across Elvis, that was purely accidental on my part, I might add; the brake shoes fell off the Hillman Minx.

Anyway, Elvis was an amateur archetype superstar. He couldn't play guitar – he had no concept of the guitar, he tried to blow into it – but he knew how to have a good time.

And back in the 1950s that was more difficult.

My influence on Elvis is immeasurable. That is, no one has ever bothered to measure it.

It was on my advice that Elvis went to Germany. He wasn't actually in the army. That was story we put out.

We wanted to change his hair style and it gave us the eighteen months we needed to get the combination of Brylcreem, Californian Poppy and bacon fat out of his hair.

That's not to say that people weren't impressed with his music. His record company were so impressed they wanted him to go to Germany – or anywhere.

Elvis, thinking Germany was just outside Memphis, accepted.

I got Elvis his recording contract. As Elvis played a medley of tunes, I held Sam Phillip's head under water until he agreed to sign him.

It was then that his music began to create no small interest that Colonel Tom Parker white-anted me.

He sent Elvis seventy cheeseburgers, eighteen gallons of Cherry Coke and a fifteen-page contract. The rest is history.

But I'm not going to exploit the Elvis legend with a kiss-and-tell book or old recordings of Elvis after a curry evening.

I want him remembered the way he really was. That's why the Rottnest Island Film Commission pharmaceutical company is releasing Elvis Drugs – uppers and downers cleverly shaped like little guitars and hound dogs.

Remember Elvis Drugs: Love Me Tenderizers and Blue Suede Ludes.

I WOULD LIKE to address your attention to the role of movie critics and their constant references to old movies.

And in this context, it's difficult not to over-estimate the value of the word 'old' when discussing Margaret Pomeranz's contribution given that she wrote the notices panning the Lumiére Brothers' film of a train coming into a station.

Of course, we do have to be sympathetic to someone like Margaret who is involved in being a (film) critic because it's an innocuous and soporific pastime.

After all, who would notice if film critics went on strike? Would the country grind to a halt? Would John Howard call in the army? Can you imagine 'The Movie Show' being presented by an SAS staff officer: 'I saw the new Bernardo Bertolucci film, *Stealing Beauty* and it was crap!'

It's an illness, this movie critic caper. You have to watch yourself carefully. It can start innocently enough by taking out too many videos, then it's a slippery slope [down] to boring people totally shitless at dinner parties with your witty repartee about how you recognised Marlon Brando's half-sister's ex-husband in the Merchant Ivory remake of Jane Austen's unpublished manuscript, *Back Door Bonanza,* [by which time] it's probably a good idea to seek 'real' help.

Otherwise, you'll be spotting Hedy Lamarr's uncle behind the tasteful set decor provided by the man who gave [it] to Liberace – the furniture that is – and screaming this information to the helpless patrons of public transport (or on the media) and sadly it's only a short hop from there to the padded room, the canvas coat that does up at the back, or a career on the ABC.

If you insist on not getting help, then I've prepared a few key facts to help you stay above the critical waterline in the pulse-quickening banter you'll need to have when you've got your snout in the trough at the gala premiere of the next award-winning, internationally-acclaimed film preview you attend.

* The greatest actor in the history of the world was Brando – or not.
* Alfred Hitchcock appeared in his own films, except the ones he didn't.
* Marilyn Monroe was misunderstood, loved Sibelius and was a brilliant actress – or not.
* Groucho Marx once said something witty about everything.
* Doris Day's real name was Robert Zimmerman and many knew her before she was a virgin.
* *Citizen Kane* is a kind of American *Muriel's Wedding*.
* And Ken Russell is a dickhead who can't direct for toffee.

When it comes to talking about films themselves, you just have to remember the all-purpose, grab-bag of critic-speak or write:

* The film retains an expression of Italian Neo-Realistic mise-en-scene.
* The director allows a build up of tension in a wry and puckish, almost mischievous way that owes a lot to – name some obscure director here – whose films are an instrument of social change and an entertainment to children.
* But that doesn't mean the film is in the least didactic. True, there is a pervasive Marxist quality to it but this – director name here again – has great success in espousing his auteurism through his subtle genre parody.
* The title is ironic and says more about our involvement in – insert collective national guilt here – than countless books by David Stratton on the subject.
* I was reminded as I left the cinema of the remarkable pronouncement – quote something you heard between your naps.
* How historically inevitable!

Now when you think of the amount of air-time and reams of newsprint these, these wankers, spend saying this, you wonder why John Howard doesn't send in the troops.

They are a waste of space, a hazard to shipping and intellectual dog turds on the lawn of artistic expression – or not.

PREPARATION [IS AFOOT] of the definitive history of the Rottnest Island Film Commission and Sir Bruce Fernargle-Jones.

Madonna [it should be noted in passing] has just released a fly-on-the-wall exposé called *In Bed with Madonna*. This Rottnest Island Film Commission doco is entitled *Around the S-Bend with Sir Bruce,* and is directed by the famous Hindi documentary filmmaker, Mustapha Cuppatee, who directed *Gidget's Suttee Experience*.

To the history then.

Around 1600, there are no mentions of the Rottnest Island Film Commission, although the 'foul apparitions' in Shakespeare's *Hamlet* and *Macbeth* are obvious references to his manager Indigo Fernargle.

Between 1642 and 1646, you had the English Civil War where career bureaucrats won over the toffee-nosed aristocrats with their silly costumes and idiot prep-school children who were brought up by nannies and packed off to boarding school to [have their] bottoms used as toast racks for the older boys.

In the 1800s, Napoleon was conquering Italy, Spain, Egypt and Austria but he always tended to avoid Rottnest.

During the Second World War, I fought with McArthur in the Philippines and Montgomery in the desert – some blokes you just can't get along with.

1945. Hitler committed suicide in Berlin having seen a proposal I sent him for the Belsen Film Commission.

In 1974, I founded the Rottnest Island Film Commission under a massive non-repayable government grant.

The Rottnest Island Film Commission Centre was opened by Her Majesty The Queen's butcher.

Two days later the Film Centre fell down. The Film Commission board members had decided that an architect was not an expendable item.

Meanwhile, the Reverend Fred Nile, aided by B.A. Santamaria announced that there were 1,447 pro-choice, communist fellow travellers employed by the Rottnest Island Film Commission.

With a government grant, I formed a committee to investigate the canteen food and the Red Menace. Sixteen million dollars later, I announced that of the 1,447 staff of the Commission, there's only Vera in the canteen who votes Labor, and while Mrs Tule, the cleaning lady, is an unreconstructed Stalinist, she actually votes Liberal.

But these findings were too late to save the Fraser government.

Anyway, Fred and B.A. were later to announce that Fraser was a communist, as were the Queen, the Pope, Sir Peter Abels and Jamie Redfern.

NOW I DON'T want to cause any sort of rift in the ranks of the Labor Party, a party whose loyalty could only be rivalled by that of the Liberal Party.

It behoves me, as something of an elder statesperson, to make some comments about the contribution of Senator Peter Walsh to the debate.

Don't think for a moment that Peter Walsh will be the leader of the Labor Party.

Or at least he won't be leader of the Labor Party for some years yet.

And if he does become leader, which Peter doesn't want [to be], I think he'll be a good leader because history tells us that leaders who become leaders, even if they're not very good, will probably be the leader.

Keating has got a solid team behind him.

Peter Walsh is in that team and Paul won't have to worry about watching his back.

Paul is governing with skill and determination and Peter agrees with me that Paul is capable of leading the Party, even into opposition.

As Peter points out: opinion polls are one thing but anyone can be popular, even Prime Ministers.

There are people in parliament, in the Senate just waiting for a chance of a safe seat in the House of Reps. People with great experience, people like... Well, Peter knows who they are.

Paul didn't go straight into the Prime Ministership, and, like Paul, Peter is someone who rattled around the party ranks and garnered a lot of support, experience and even knowledge.

Peter thinks we should go with a proven leader, but the proven leader has gone to work at Channel Nine.

So we've got a leader whose appeal is well-known but is not a well-known leader.

Peter and I support Paul. He should have the job. He's the leader. I just hope Peter realises you've got to be behind the leader.

I suppose he does because that's the best place if you're going to stick in the knife.

KIM BEAZLEY, THE Minister of Defence, has resolved in the new year not to call the navy out at night by itself, [to provide] a new box of bullets for the army, and that we'll have an air force.

Kylie Minogue has resolved to pick up her studies in Cartesian Dualism and finish reading a book without any pictures in it.

Russ Hinze is giving up nouvelle cuisine. He doesn't think two carrot sticks and a gerbil chop is dinner. Now he's really going to get stuck into his tucker.

Mike Gorbachev is resolved to remain everyone's favourite uncle. So we'll have to find a new enemy. How about those Garfield cats on suction cups in car windows? I like to 'nuke' them!

Den Chou Ping has resolved to legitimate political protest with murderous frenzy rather than the concessions of 1989.

Imelda Marcos, I asked, but she pelted me with about two thousand shoes when I stuck my head over the fence.

Generals Pinochet and Noriega – same resolution. They would like the CIA to come in and put them and all their country's money in an airplane and fly off and live rich in Miami.

Renewed hunger in Africa has inspired Rex Piranha, car dealer and accountant, and Nakkaga Nebibi, along with other pre-owned car dealers, to organise Lemon Aid. They've resolved to give enormous discounts on sun-roofs and sports packs to starving motorists.

Political mates down at the Alan Bond America's Cup Souvenir Stand and Merchant Bank have resolved to initiate Federal Aid in 1990. All our aborigines suffering polio, leprosy and other diseases unknown in the rest of the Australian community will get shaving kits, eye shades, slippers, movie head sets and small hot towels as given away on first-class flights.

Reverend Jim Christian Goofbucket has made a resolution before God, his Swiss bank manager, to build an amusement park, look after old folks' pension money and clog Sunday morning TV with shows that tell children that dinosaurs died last week. All to the greater glory of his name.

A LOT OF YOUNG, bewildered, confused people stop me in the street.

Now I lump young people, mental patients and members of rock 'n' roll bands together in one subcategory of humanity.

All have an enduring tradition of weird clothes– which helps we adults to avoid them.

It is difficult to escape their frequent stupid fads and constant emotional problems.

Young people are drawn to me and ask the same questions. They write to you, Robert, again with the same burning question: 'Are you my dad?' They ask, 'How am I going to meet someone?' Someone who'll grow to like them enough to handle their genitals.

And as boring as young people are, they are sufficiently impressed with themselves to want to impose their ignorant little selves on some other devil in a biological Clash of the Titans, and call it a relationship!

Young people who might be having a 'relationship' must realise that they are not supposed to go out with anyone except their new 'partner' for a few weeks at least.

It allows adults and parents an opportunity to get over the disgust of the thought of them together.

Of course, locations have been provided for the young folk to meet each other.

Appropriately, they're dark, smell, dingy venues with loud, ear-shattering, throbbing, audio wall paper masquerading as entertainment.

Just the place to judge a prospective partner you can't hear, see or speak to but they will fall into four distinct categories.

1 People you like more than they like you.

2 People who like you more than you like them.

3 Fools.

4 People just like your Mum and Dad.

Of course, young people, none of these are the people you're looking for but you can make them over in your fevered imagination to be a person exactly like yourself.

I'D LIKE TO have a word or two about the more memorable events in Moscow.

Now, in the Land of Our Powerful Friend, the top job in recent years is beginning to be determined by central casting.

Recently the lead role in the American Dream has been secured by George Bush, taking over from the semi-retired Ron Reagan.

Which is akin to Trigger taking over from Roy Rodgers.

Now, as we are acutely aware, Mike 'Splotch' Gorbachev has decided to get out of the family business and spend some time with the family– as his video suggests.

Admittedly, last week it was [a] decision Mike wouldn't have made at all.

A few people down at the party headquarters took it into their heads to show Mike, with the aid of the ever-effective Soviet re-education [system?], the T-34 tank, that he was a making a mistake dedicating what possibly remained of his life to politics.

Mike found the track a bit heavy. He didn't understand the Soviet economic legacy. That is, we pretend to pay you and you pretend to work.

With this latest resignation, Mike, in all fairness, seems to have got the idea as it was announced.

Now the only problem is – who gets the souvenir key-ring and matching keys that can blow us all to radio-active cinderland?

When I spoke to Mike, he didn't have them. He could have left them on the deli counter at the GUM store.

Did he lock them in the missile silo? – and the RAC [is having] a devil of a time using a coat hanger to break in.

Were they in the milk bottle?

Have the kids hidden them?

Of course, when Leonid Brezhnev was getting on a bit and showing signs of too many aluminium saucepans, they gave him a sonic key-ring. Being the cutting edge of soviet technology, it [was] concealed in something the size of a soccer ball.

At least when Mike came along, they did leave emergency instructions on how to hot-wire Armageddon. Attach your ignition wire to the battery, short out the terminals in the starter motor, after grovelling under the dash...

And there you have it: Armageddon.

Mike's a smart man. He's pinpointed his position and put in his order for a paddle long ago. Now, with the old guard out, we might just join him up that well-known tributary.

I'D LIKE TO have a word about the wonderful world of trade sanctions.

I know there's a lot of ignorant peons out there who don't have the privilege of sitting on the right hand of government.

So while Paul's out of the country, I feel it has fallen to me to give you a full run-down on precisely what we're doing or thinking of doing.

In an effort to orchestrate a concerted response to Libya, the Europeans and Americans have put their money some distance from their mouths and imposed sanctions – except for the bit of Libya they want. That is, the oily bits.

Australia, in our established role as the vanguard of over-reaction and total confusion, and we alone, have complied with the European Economic Community and the United States of America to the letter.

We've looked at our trade with Libya and sanctioned it.

That's because we're measured and responsible. That is, we measure it in votes and we're responsible to the United States and their European chums.

The Australian government believes that, in the interest of all countries, we must bring home to the Libyans food and medical supplies that are the exceptions, along with their oil, to indicate that their behaviour is rejected by the family of nations. Well, by Europe and the United States.

And *they* certainly wouldn't behave like a bunch of terrorist unless it was absolutely necessary to do so.

Especially in bombing the *Rainbow Warrior* or an unjustified and massive air strike on Tripoli and associated civilians.

And as Mum says: 'Don't do as I do, do as I say'.

THE PUBLIC ARE the very people who vote in an election.

And only last weekend we saw an example of who'd they vote for if an election was held between elections where circumstances where they (the voters) could vote for whoever they liked, and it didn't matter because it was a real election.

So what if the successful candidate hadn't spent millions on a huge election campaign devised by six CD over an open-ended, one-to-one sample with storyboard one lunch time in Bangkok?

So what if the electors of Wills found it possible to elect a bloke on the basis that he kicked goals on a Saturday and seemed like not a bad sort of bloke.

And they did this in spite of having the hand-picked leadership of the two major parties crawling up their every orifice in the run-up to polling day.

All right, let's face it. In the end, it doesn't matter how you go about getting elected – that's up to him.

But what's he going to do when someone asks him a question in the house?

Will he have the confidence to immediately accuse the other person of distorting the issue, or attempting to make cheap political capital?

No, he'll turn around and answer the question.

What's he going to do when the other members rise to speak?

Do you think Mr Cleary is going to have the parliamentary experience to go to sleep or to shout 'Rubbish!'?

No, he'll just sit there, listen intently and make the occasional intelligent, worthwhile comment.

It's obvious that Mr Cleary is going to make no contribution to the life of the parliament because he's the kind of a bloke who's never wanted to run away and join the circus.

GRAHAM TOLD ME that he's decided to get out of the business and spend some time the family.

This is not a euphemism for the New South Wales right of the party.

This was not suggested by the Keating family or the Packer family, and at no time had Graham been in contact with the Baldwin family.

In fact, Graham tells me that this is not a decision he has made recently at all.

Graham's always believed that if a job's worth doing, it's worth half-doing. Take a leaf out of his cousin-in-law's book there.

Graham said to me, 'Sir Bruce, I am not going to deny that I've found the track a [bit] heavy in the last few weeks.' And he's a little over his fighting weight.

The business immigration wasn't the success it might have been, given the reference was meant to get rid of the bugger. Graham doesn't understand the meaning of the word *immigration* as opposed to *emigration*.

In the Senate, Graham found himself pushing all manner of things up an inclination, and it was an inclination Paul wasn't prepared to adopt or manner [*sic*] he was prepared to embrace.

So Graham's dug in and is prepared to wait for better weather.

He pinpointed his position on the map just in case his loyal buddies in the right forget where he is.

And I believe that he's put in a requisition to Bob Hawke for a paddle as long ago as the last guarantee he gave about leadership challenges.

DEATH IS NOT unlike many other social events.

For example: it's not unlike marriage, especially mine.

Death can be quite chic, particularly if the dead person is a rich relative who's pegged out and left you enough money to be fashionable.

We at the Rottnest Island Film Commission Funeral Service understand death – now that we've finally had a customer.

For a while there I thought we would have to go out and shoot somebody to get it started.

For example: many people should consider dying young. It allows us at the Rottnest Island Film Commission Funeral Service to create a livelier, more with-it funeral.

Having been in the dear departed game for a while now, there are a few rules I'd like to share with young players.

1 Make sure the departed is actually dead. You won't want them half embalmed only to find out they're taking a mid-arvo snooze.

2 If they've departed to the infinite twilight home in the sky, tie up the book and movie rights. Even Lindy Chamberlain did that.

3 Don't ignore the possibility of merchandising the dead one. Particularly if they were young, well-known and died of drugs. Where would the families of Hendrix and Morrison be without this advice? Joan Crawford's daughter didn't take my advice and kissed a fortune in wire coat hangers goodbye. Dame Zara missed out on exclusive line in swimwear when Harold took the big trawl.

KEITH WILSON, the Minister for Health in Western Australia recently spent sixty-five thousand dollars of that state's crippled budget on a campaign to advise the young of the key to sexual behaviour.

It's not equality – it's simply learning to say 'no'.

When Keith was a young Anglican, about the time of Reformation, a young man would, when taking a woman out, pick her up from her home, cut up her food, tie her shoe laces, put her on his shoulders to see the parade or provide any service you would provide for a child or a trained monkey.

Obviously, fondling a knee or any other part of the lady's anatomy was definitely unheard of – actually, uninvented.

What worries Keith is that these days the barriers have all been lowered, role confusion abounds. What do you do with a male friend in a skirt in any of the aforementioned situations?

You say 'No!'.

Keith was worried that young people saw sex as the only point in dating.

Keith doesn't want young people to rush into it. The 'it's okay to say no' campaign runs a bit short on detail after this point.

So, I'm stepping in – if you will excuse the expression – to flesh it out a bit.

Do not, young people, grab hold of each other. And fondling each other's parts in front of parental bodies [is a] big No-no.

Instead, you should talk to the parents and fondle them a bit before you leave.

Sex without a relationship is tantamount to treating people like objects. Another big No-no.

People shouldn't be treated like objects; they aren't that valuable

A lot of people have intimate moments after a meal. That's a No-No! Keith and I consider that it's good form to leave the restaurant first. Saying 'no', Keith and I think you should leave with the best possible memories of your first sexual encounter.

Because the first in our society is usually the last.

NOW, I'VE BEEN given to understand that there have been rumours flying about the place that the rock that is the Anglican Church in Australia has not been answering the helm, if I may mix the metaphor.

I know there are a lot of people who would like nothing more than to see me sufficiently dragged over the theological coals, the hot coals of damnation, over this woman business.

For many years I have offered theological advice to many respected organisations in the God-bothering caper.

As you know, I'm close to 'head honchos' of the biggest multi-national prayer-fest organisers.

I have to warn some Anglicans that the supply of dark-skinned, circumcised, Jewish males who were once Red Sea fishermen or Roman tax collectors prepared to go into the Anglican ministry is getting mighty thin.

Of course, they won't see this and there will be many resignations...

But what are they going to do? Have the Anglican Church classified by the National Trust and open on Wednesdays and public holidays, so bus-loads of schoolkids and pensioners can come and stare at it?

I was told that a majority agreed with [the] ordination [of] women. Apparently, it's relatively painless and involves no sharp objects.

Even when it came to a vote – which is an idea that even God isn't crazy about – people started running in all directions.

The important thing is not that most people might not object to women as priests or that why this is an issue at all. The important thing is that those running the Anglican Church stay running the Anglican Church.

The system would be eaten away and where would Anglicans have to turn?

They can't turn to the Supreme Head of the Church on Earth, her Majesty Queen Elizabeth II – because she's a woman!

FIRST THERE WAS Ron and Nancy – They from Washington.

Ron was the first semi-retired President of the United States, who enjoyed naps and giving missiles to fanatical Middle Eastern types called Saddam.

Nancy was housewife with an interest in drugs.

Then there was George, a full-time, semi-retired ex-director of the CIA, and his wife Barbara, who had an interest in nothing at all.

Both these couples competed against the Gorbachev family of Moscow, Union of Soviet Socialist Republics.

Mike worked as a secretary (although his shorthand was not the best) for the USSR's prestigious Communist Party [which was] formed after everyone not in the Party was shot.

In his spare time, Mike, or 'Splotch-top' as we called him, liked to have games of *Glasnost* or, as his buddies in the Polit Bureau and the military like to call it, consequences.

Mike's lovely wife, Raisa, enjoyed making Nancy and Barbara look like the ignorant peons they were.

Mike broke a lot of conventions. He stopped killing or imprisoning all the smart people, popular since 1917. He stopped scaring the crap out of everyone while building hydro-electric plants where there weren't any rivers.

He put an end to the all-expenses-paid potato harvest.

And declared that the Soviet Union was a museum of the drab, the irksome and the things made of concrete.

Mike tore down the Wall but George didn't confess he was kidding about SDI.

Thanks to *perestroika*, it was to be the new Gorby-era Soviet life style – with squeals of glee coming from the Gulags.

Splotch-top changed the place.

When Brezhnev was about things weren't too flash. Speak out of turn, and it was electrodes attached to the reproductive organs.

Under Mike, the Soviet citizens got litter. Under Brezhnev, there was nothing to litter with!

Mike gave them more cars. Rush hour in Moscow is almost like nine o'clock on a Sunday in Yapoon.

OVER THE PAST week, you may have caught the ranting of a polo buddy of mine on the google-box.

No [not], Jana Wendt, but she *was* talking to another old pal of mine, Kerry (I'll sell it to you for a billion and get it back for a lot less) Packer.

Kerry was telling [talking to?] the incisive, incredibly well-paid, hard-nosed, probing Miss Wendt, who happens to work for Kerry in an unbiased capacity.

Kerry pointed out that it had been two years since the staff of *The Herald* and *The Age* newspapers had a 'real' boss.

And what had they done in all [this time] without a Kerry or a Warwick or a Rupert? They [had] carried on putting out a quality tabloid.

That's harsh, almost personal, criticism from a man like Kerry.

Are these people at *The Age* or *The Herald* big enough to take this much flak?

How far do they think they're going to get putting out newspapers that tell stories that people with a modicum of intelligence can understand?

Who needs politics, economics, the state of the nation? These go on for hours like this, and reading, it's impossible to get any idea of what's actually happening to the burning issues: is Elvis really in the submarine with Harold or is he just a deckhand? Has a UFO really sucked Kylie off the planet? Has intelligent life been found in the opposition's Shadow Cabinet?

And when did *The Age* or *The Herald* ever have Bob's home phone number?

So much for *their* influence!

THE ROTTNEST ISLAND Film Commission has agreed to break into the lucrative market of rock 'n' roll.

Eric Fossil is our big hope in the mega-star category.

Although he had a bit of a set-back when he fell over recently. He was trying to stand up when the accident occurred.

But Eric's fans have no need to worry. It won't delay the release of his manager Rex Piranha, who's nearly served his time.

Eric, as you know, is the lead drinker and guitarist for 'The Nasties' and he's fallen off stage in every major city in the United States. He's currently recovering from an overdose of doctors.

Our heavy metal band, 'Dead Monkeys', are to split up. They've been in the business ten years now, nine as other groups.

Originally, they were 'Dead Salmon'. They became for a while 'Trout', then 'Fried Trout', then 'Poached Trout in a White Wine Sauce', then 'Dead Loss', and lately 'Dead Monkeys'.

Ronnie Amphetamine represented the Rottnest Island Film Commission's big break-through artist – in the legend stakes at least.

He'll be up there with the greats: Elvis, John Lennon, Jim Morrison...

He's the first all-dead rock star. We'll fly his body around the world, following the international success of his post-mortem appearance 'In Concrete'.

Admittedly, we've kept him on ice for a few years but his 'Rigour Mortis' album was still solid in the charts.

And we're releasing Paul McCartney – you know the famous Paul McCartney – of 'The Davenport Brothers'.

We're releasing his dalliance with classical music: a 'War Requiem'. Recorded live, it lasted for four hours and used two orchestras and nearly a thousand tons of explosive.

It's resulted in four recording contracts, a film deal, one hundred and thirty-seven dead and eighty-four missing presumed killed.

But that's showbiz.

I DON'T WANT to be accused of over-reacting here but there have been some unfortunate remarks made about those selfless, dedicated and patriotic people who control banking in the wide brown thing of ours.

Some people still niggle about that sensible decision over charges for cheques and other bank services.

Whose business is it anyway? They're not running a shop, you know.

I'm surprised the banks tell their customers about what they're charged for.

Charges are completely justified – more or less.

Banks provide services to their customers. Not all, just the ones who've got more of the banks money than the bank.

It's those ordinary investors – home owners, small business types. They've been abusing the system for years. They open a cheque account, then – blow me down – they sit right down a write a whole lot of cheques.

A cheque account is only a kick-off for a whole range of charges to come into effect.

Otherwise, you'd be putting your money in an account where it can't be got at in anything under a light year and only [for] which the banks pay you interest.

Interest on cheque accounts simply means if your account is overdrawn they (the bank) charge interest as well as the charges, and it charges charges to the interest – if you had any – which you don't, because it's been eaten away, being only microscopic to start with.

Which is only fair.

TONIGHT I'D LIKE to have a few words about some of the men who single-handedly...

Well, not exactly single-handedly because there is more than one of them.

Anyway, they are the people who prevent the media and its associated hacks from having to admit that there's no news.

People like Michael Jackson. 'Is he blowing bubbles?' the Forth estate enquires.

Has Howard Hughes died for the fourth time?

Is Elvis really in command of Harold Holt's submarine?

Tonight I'd like to refer to a beauty of a story about someone who'd hit the headlines every month every time someone dug up chicken scraps in the Berlin suburbs.

But I'm here to tell you that well-known storm trooper, the man who held Hitler's coat during the hostilities of 39-45, Martin Boorman is alive.

In fact, the Rottnest Island Film Commission has entered a conjunctive [sic] development with Martin's building company.

Now there is some possibility that he isn't Martin Boorman. He's missing a scar and hasn't got Martin Boorman's teeth.

Now, as I see it, the scar was never there or it might have come off.

But the teeth are a worry. If he hasn't got Martin Boorman's teeth, who has?

Anyway, we're building a new hotel on the site of some of Rottnest's most famous buildings.

Marty's got some great ideas:

Guests will arrive in the Appeasement Hall;

Special staff will make sure you have no complaints;

Breakfast will be in the tropic splendour of the Mengele Room;

Or you can relax in the Lebensraum Room;

Or take the Luftwaffe lift to the Anschluss Bar and be served racially pure cocktails by our brown-shirted barmen;

Then back to the Appeasement Hall after your stay for the final solution of your bill.

Marty just wanted to ask any of his pals living quietly in Australia to pop in if they needed a job.

NOW, I'VE NOTICED in the rags that your compatriots in the fourth estate are soon to be owned exclusively by that red-raggin', pinko, commo, Kerry Francis Bullmore Packer.

Anyway, journalists and the concerned public – not to be confused with the 'totally couldn't give a monkey's' public – have missed the point.

There is a tendency to bring into question our policy of tacit support for the Indonesian hounding of the East Timorese.

Now, let me say, as I reiterated last week in Djakarta, that Australia's response to the events in Dili is not to make it a flashpoint in the region but rather we have to be measured and responsible.

Bob said, when I got back from delivering the AIDEX free sample of ammunition to the Indonesian military, 'Sir Bruce, before we react, we have to measure the votes and be responsible to Washington'.

We have to take a strong stand in and around the general area of money.

We've been accused of being inconsistent here, but look at the evidence. Money is the one area of our dealings with the Indonesians where we've been consistent in everything we've done.

There's no point in refusing to sell stuff to the Indonesians. They'll just go out and buy from someone else who'd like our market. Like the Americans.

It would be like the Gulf Crisis all over again.

We'd make the grand moral gesture in support of Freedom.

And the Americans would come in on our Indonesian markets to make some fairly grand amounts of money.

If we're not going to sell Indonesian weapons of destruction, we're only sabotaging our own economic well-being.

We've got to ban the sale of items that they can't get from elsewhere, which will frustrate and confuse them as a nation and a people.

OVER THE PAST few weeks our audience – which must amount to a small number of people – must have been considering: where is Sir Bruce Fernargle-Jones?

Why haven't his dulcet tones been on the Bakerlite?

I've been cosseted away with John Hewson and the lads of the Shadow Cabinet, putting the finishing touches to the only solution in our hands – the other way out of the hole we've got ourselves in: A consumption tax.

And I thought you, the audience, would rather hear it here first, from a friend.

Well, [when] Paul, I mean John, first ran it past me, my immediate reaction was; what have those poor little consumptives done to deserve this?

But Paul, I mean, John said that the problem was, generally speaking, that Australians use money for consumption not investment.

Paul and John said we need investment in this country.

We've tried to get the Japanese and the Americans interested but they still don't own the place, and as a last resort, we're going to have to get Australians to do it themselves.

So, I see the consumption tax as a consultancy fee the government charges for their guidance in matters of investment.

Therefore, all consumption will be regarded as borrowings from the government.

But as Paul points out, but John hasn't bothered to point out as yet: all that consumption is primarily of imported bits and pieces from Japan and America, which is probably why they didn't buy the rest of the place.

And only a consumption tax will be like interest on the consultancy fees that we're charged for guidance from the government.

I'd better let John know what Paul said there; you know what they're like – a bit of information and its back to 'we'll give our overall philosophy as soon as we get one' time.

ABOUT THESE AMOUNTS of money I'm supposed to have received from various pals in the merchant banking game.

And before we go any further, I want to repudiate any connection with the credit company run by me or my pals, God Will Pay Plastic Company, or American Excess.

It was not my idea; it was a facility made available to me.

American Excess operated like any normal credit card, except that I could only use it where no one else was using the service.

For example, I'd walk up to an airline and say, 'Many people travelling first-class?' They'd say, 'No'. I'd say, 'I'll put it on my American Excess.'

At the end of the month, I'll admit I never received an account, just a brown paper bag carried by PPS [?].

This refund, I admit, I did obtain, although it wasn't $25,000, it was $25.00.

The house I was given on the Gold Coast was actually an apartment.

The boat should more correctly been referred to as an ocean-going yacht. And it didn't have a fake keel – it was real.

I don't even own it! It's owned by a hire company that my wife is not very much a director of.

Now, as for Brian, Bob and Laurie.

Bob never had anything invested with Laurie except as it turns out his political future and that of the ALP.

Perhaps he was looking for a safe investment to protect the little man.

And it's unfortunate that we can't find the little man.

But Brian assures us that Laurie didn't ask Bob until Bob said Laurie said he asked him. On or before the date that he therefore didn't mislead anyone or parliament.

And if that's what Bob said he said to Laurie. If in fact he said anything at all to Laurie on that small boat – apart from get your hands off my tackle – then I'm prepared to give him the benefit of the doubt. Or not, depending on what Bob just said.

THERE'S BEEN A Lot of talk about Sir Ninian Stephen being hand-picked to head the Northern Ireland peace initiative.

But I'm here to tell you that Sir Nin was their first choice.

At the moment, [as] the British officials call it, there's 'an acceptable level of violence' afoot in the province.

But what's not acceptable to you, me or Sir Nin? Well, not 'excellent' the way it was in 1972, 1916, 1798, or 1690 but 'fair-to-middling' for a province half the size of Victoria with a population smaller than Brisbane.

As for the violence being levelled, it's the usual indiscriminate automatic weapons fire, knee-cappings, discovery of arms caches and attacks with 'devices' (as they are known) made out of tin soldiers and Dad's hanky, and, of course, the ever-popular car bombs (an Irish invention).

Successive British governments have had a go at keeping the Protestant homicidal maniacs away from the Catholic murderers.

Of course, Sir Nin will have to fight his way through the hordes of social scientists. There's not a local resident who isn't a footnote on somebody's Master's thesis.

The Irish have got a lot to learn about slums though. No homeless living in garbage bags, no crack houses, no six-foot hairy-legged transvestites with knives, no heroin addicts.

The IRA shoots them all.

Sir Nin's plan will probably be different to mine. I favoured thundering around in a personnel carrier, levelling weapons from all hatches at all and sundry. It seemed to lack that personal touch that I perceived the Brits and the Irish wanted.

So I volunteered Sir Nin.

Lady Fernargle-Jones is knitting Sir Nin a flak jacket or an armoured personnel carrier.

EASTER HOLIDAYS.

Lady Fernargle-Jones and I think about a special friend of the family. Like you, Rob [but not you].

He's the kind of bloke, a man after my own heart, liver and spleen, who attempts to lift the popular morale of the international community against the miasma of apathy and pools of despond into which our planet – this fragment of solar driftwood – has descended.

Of course, I am talking about the former concrete sub-contractor, retired actor and international jet-setter, Karl Wojtyla.

Kazza, as he's known at our place, has [had] a tough trot, working at Easter and Christmas.

When he arrives at airports, Kazza is always down there, checking out how well laid the 'grano [?]' work was; the only opportunity he gets to experience a good lay.

As Kazza says, 'Just because I don't play the game, doesn't mean I can't make the rules'.

Many is the time I've been out on Kazza's wonderful renaissance balcony – part of the Michaelangelo add-on to the Vatican – in front of a thronging multitude.

You can get more people in Saint Peter's Square than are owed money by state financial institutions where Labor holds power.

Then Kazza and I go and indulge in *his* favourite recreational pastime: fishing.

Being an unmarried man, he has more time to wrestle with the tackle.

Kazza, in a quiet reflective moment, asked me [about] taking on the position.

My plans for the Vatican:

* holy water slide,
* painting the Sistine Chapel (which is too busy) a duck-egg blue,
* Pope mobile dodgems in Saint Peter's Square,
* audience with Brian Burke.

[I HAVE BEEN] checking out the possibility of being ambassador to Ireland.

[It was an] itinerary [that] was exhaustive and included Paris, Marseilles and Gibraltar.

And then back to Paris to pick up Lady Fernarge-Jones from the left luggage at Charles De Gaulle Airport.

[Then] onto Lake Como, some Alps, the Pyramids, the Holy Lands, the grandeur that was Rome and the pile of volcanic ash that was Pompeii.

Did the Louvre, copped an optic at Mont Blanc and pondered the eternal riddle: where'd the nose of the Sphinx go?

As an Australian ambassador, I know that all races, creeds and colours understand English when it's spoken loudly and clearly.

There are some locales that a career diplomat would not want. [Places] full of 'experienced travellers': Angola, Eritrea, Bangladesh, for example.

There you are, pinned down by mortar fire in the middle of a genocide atrocity and through it all comes six law partners and their wives in bush jackets, having 'an experience' and wanting the Embassy to change their visas.

They get upset and in a snit when the natives won't make a steak *frite* out of the family water buffalo.

Some may point at Brian but this is the life he faced in the job.

Diplomacy has lost a lot of it dignity and that's his reason for wanting to get out.

I don't think people realise it's a life full of intrigue.

And things are never as they seem. Paper bag [?]

So take Brian's word if you're in politics and want a career in diplomacy: drop bread or cut blazes in trees so can back out, embarrassing no-one, while [?when] you realise all the native bearers have turned to working for someone else.

OODNARGARLARBI, THE QUEEN City of the Drought-stricken West, was hostess to the Second Annual Rottnest Island Film Commission Awards - the Golden Claws.

Many people across this wide brown land watched via Quokka-sat as I bid them welcome to the glittering ballroom of the Railway Hotel.

Of course, I welcomed many luminaries and celebrities as President of the Australian Society of Motions, Pictures and Arts. Having Robert would have made it go off.

What a galah occasion it was to have former Deputy Premier of Western Australia, David Parker, in the audience along with Australia's Mr TV, Hector Crawford.

Miss Julie was the hostess and barrel-girl for the evening.

Dolly Dyer was going to do the job but she's been busy baby-sitting the marlin.

I had a terribly hard time finding winners this year because we had a hard time finding the film industry.

Nominated best film were:

Home Alone, the story of a charismatic female premier with hamstring problems and the situation she finds herself in after a Royal Commission has done in her cabinet colleagues and her mandate from the masses;

Dances With Wombats, the Leyland Brothers with warm, furry things;

Harold (Part 1): You Can't Round Corners;

Stormin' Norman Pulls it Off.

Other best films were Agfa, Ilford and Kodak – all receiving enormous assistance from the Federal Government and they all promised to move [to] or stay in the Prime Minister's electorate.

Best Actress nominations went to Maggie Taberra, Googie Withers and Margaret Fulton.

Surprise winner in this category and Best Actor, Best Screenplay Adaptation, Editing and Foreign Language Film went to Wimpy, the piano-playing marsupial.

Best Original Score went to my secretary Miss Susie Goodhead.

Film and television production has never been lower than now.

What we need is more local content. Through the Rottnest Island Film Commission and the annual Golden Claws, [we are doing] what John Kerr did to parliamentary democracy.

AS YOU KNOW, the Rottnest Island Film Commission, in its role as an entrepreneurial statutory body of the island, has ventured into many fields.

I thought as there's an ongoing debate in this wide brown thing about the need for proper education, I'd give you a run-down of *our* independent school, Saint Joan the Burnt, sister school of Saint Elvis.

Australia needs to become a clever country. At the moment in the family of nations, it's down behind the dunnies having a smoke.

Saint Joan the Burnt is blazing a path for education in Australia.

Any independent school can claim to produce its share of doctors, lawyers, engineers, bankrupts and radio celebrities, but at Saint Joan's, we're committed to filling the gap.

And that's a big problem – it's a wide gap. One that this nation is groaning under the strain to fill.

Our curriculum is designed to produce the merchant bankers, the right-wing, free market Labor Party leaders, the foreign national media tycoons and telephone desanitizers of the future.

Staffing at Saint Joan's draws on a wide experiential basis; a staff dedicated to thrusting into the cognitive void:
*   Richard Nixon – political theory and audio engineering;
*   John Kerr – constitutional law and bar management;
*   Chris Skase – media studies and self-defence;
*   Any Triple J announcer – spoken English;
*   Saddam Hussein – geography;
*   General Managers of the State Banks of South Australia, Victoria and Western Australia – economics;
*   Yul Brynner and Rock Hudson – a Health Education wing to be opened next year.

I SHOULD POINT out more or less from the beginning that not everyone can shoot.

The demands made on the human brain can be so intense that only profoundly intelligent people of sensitive disposition can cope at all.

As I talk, if you close your eyes and imagine that you're a piece of native fauna or at a suburban shopping precinct, you'll get some idea how high-powered weapons are only played with by the cleverest people.

First, you should obtain a weapon. (You should take notes. This is where it gets technical.)

Then you should learn to load the weapon. Imagine the excitement this causes amongst the intelligentsia.

Even – even – [Jean-Paul Sartre?] found this a hard concept to grapple with.

It was only when Simone de Beauvoir made the comparison with Ludo did this famous French philosopher get a rough idea with regard to the existential implications.

Now, once you've got the feel for your weapon, or, as Sigmund Freud once said to Carl Jung, while stalking the occupants of an office block: 'The ante-nocturnal, pre-micturitunal prey syndrome happening'.

Of course, Anna Freud, with her obsessions with sex, described that as [the] 'post-going-back-to-your-place-for-a-bit-of-loin-gratification reflex'.

John Stuart Mill, like a thinking genius, and farmers realised firing shotguns folds your arms nearly around [your] back in a manner made famous by ducks – coincidently.

Shooting is not a barbaric caper carried on my psychotic sociopaths with desires to exert their feeble personalities upon the world through weapons of death, and if you don't believe me ask this man...

I AM STILL ON QUOK-SAT 1.

Bob Hawke, on whose hand I sit, has asked me to monitor an exciting exchange programme.

Politicians for hostages!

Swapping Gough Whitlam – what a swap!

Saddam Hussein is getting some top notch Australian diplomats, Federal and State representatives in return for skilled Iranian crafts people.

People could write in nominating.

Imagine what Peter Dowding and Brian Burke could do for the Iraqi economy.

You've probably heard the music from Wimpy, the keyboard playing marsupial.

I've been up here for two weeks, listening to this creature pounding away on the ivories.

Of course, Earth-orbiting isn't all beer and skittles, you now.

I've had to step out of Quokka-Sat 1 and change the Van Allen Belt a dozen times.

I have to admit that I'm getting a bit bored up here: 'The planet Earth is blue and there's nothing I can do'.

The oxygen and rations are running a bit low and Wimpy and I are taking alternative breaths and drinking each other's urine.

I am quite looking forward to a bit of re-entry.

[AN INSIGHT INTO] real estate agents.

They pressure their kids to be chartered accountants, senior policemen, used car vendors or child molesters.

Real Estate Agents have an important job. They have to beat-up the price of something without adding absolutely anything in any meaningful way.

Real Estate Agents have to look a certain way: crotch-grabbing bri-nylon business suits, matched with chunky gold jewellery, a totally undetectable hair-piece and five o'clock shadow.

And that's just the women!

Language: a vivid imagination and total contempt for the trade practices and consumer protection acts in your various states and territories also helps.

Real Estate language usage –

Spacious: cat-swinging could become a recreational possibility.

Tasteful: carpeted, painted and curtained by someone not rendered tasteless by God.

Leafy aspects: means that the garden is probably inhabited by friends of Diane Fossey.

Near public transport: means a freeway passes within six feet of the bedroom window.

Full of character: every time you flush the dunny the garage doors fall off.

Investment opportunity: means you should seriously propose marriage to Janet Holmes-a-Court.

Absolute water frontage: means you should stock up on sandbags and keep the furniture in the ceiling.

Beautifully presented: none of the neighbours has thrown up in the letter box.

Handy to shops: suggests Burke and Wills had a better chance of finding sustenance.

Prime location: close to the kind of industrial activity that'll give your kids three heads.

Park-like garden: full of child molesters, broken bottle and dog turds.

Character home: designed by the inmates of a mental hospital.

[YOU] MAY DISAGREE with me. Bill Hayden became emotional – he'd been in the party, man-and-boy, for forty-three years.

Labor's been well served by these long-timers, Jack Eggleton and John Kerr.

Bob! How could he undermine his socialist principles? A man who presided over the wages breakout of the early 1970s and the reduction [of] real wages in the 1980s.

I stepped in. I told the delegates of Fernargle-Jones's master plan.

Not only should we deregulate the Commonwealth Bank, Australian Airlines, and QANTAS, but what about deregulating the government?

This is a democracy. Why can't free enterprise set up in opposition to the bunch of power-crazed amateurs who sit, divorced from reality, in their ivory tower?

Let's get incentive into area such as welfare, tax and defence.

Imagine a welfare system that returned a profit.

Get free enterprise to pay the dole. After all they're the ones not employing them.

Defence. An army, navy and air force that could shoot its way into the black. What's the point of having them if they're not all dying for us – and it's in their contracts.

Law is there for the protection of the people. Just imagine how much safer you'd be if you could top up the protection. Admittedly it's a pilot scheme that's been operating in a few states, until *Four Corners* blew the gaff.

If the thinking people of Australia were alive today, they'd want me to go for it.

The conference wasn't too impressed but when your back's to the wall, you can only go forward – to the next wall.

[I HAVE BEEN engaged in] shuttle diplomacy. [There has been a] need [to do so?] with taxpayers' funds to revive Rottnest Island Film Commission Airlines.

[We have] picked up a second-hand Air New Zealand airbus [which has had] only one flight via scenic Antarctica.

Iraqis are [a] fairly dangerous bunch of people who can't be trusted with anything more sophisticated than a fountain pen. Hussein may stick that in your eye.

Now, if ordinary folk said this, [they'd] wind up on a string in the airport gift shop.

Russians and Americans, who aren't as happy as we first thought, have suddenly noticed that they [are] getting the attention of the world's media because *they* aren't going to be the ones to turn it into a radioactive cinder in one of the [outer?] spiral arms of the galaxy.

France – with the morals of a happy rabbit.

India - with no privation among its population has every reason to spend billions.

Israel - which has got a bomb, which it *hasn't* been testing.

None of these countries noticed President Hussein at the check-out when they were picking up nuclear bits and pieces.

Nobody thought that the six million dollars President Hussein spent [on] nuclear fission/chips/wingnuts could be used for anything else but camel pacifiers.

We wouldn't do that sort of thing. What's a bit of yellowcake between old mates like the French and Hawke?

The only problem with sitting on Bob's right hand is you can't tell what his left one's up to.

[I HAVE BEEN] wondering what to do with the ABC.

It didn't come to me when confronted with this glittering array of technology I have before me.

It was when I discovered that the Corporation had a $350 million budget.

Now, this would have to be the Everest of quasi-autonomous, statutory, governmental bodies.

Just imagine what Sir Bruce Fernargle-Jones could do with, sorry, to this August Tribal Drum of the Antipodes. And drum-banging [is] something I've had a go at from time to time.

We had statistics done, [had] more commissions than the ABC Radio [*indecipherable*] God has had blood tests, and finally Kim 'Rambo' Beazley, the King Kong of telecommunications in this country, turned to me and said, 'Sir Bruce, it's all got to come to a head! Give it a squeeze and put the Clearasil of your guiding hand on this eczema of the national estate.'

So, I've come up with/burst out with a plan to rationalise the operations here at the ABC, in line with the current ALP policy, which no-one seems to be able to find, and Bob and the right-wing couldn't give a toss about anyway.

What's a party platform for if you can't sit around the Lodge with Kerry and Peter Abels and have a laugh about it?

I digress. We're planning to put the ABC employees in uniforms designed by Lady Fernargle-Jones and make a commercial about them being excited – like Australian Airlines and the Armed Forces.

[We will] change its name to Channel Ten and get Westpac to give us a heap of folding stuff that we can chuck up against the wall. And get away with 'cause we're a private company.

The ABC couldn't do that, now could they?

Of course, we could make perceptive, expensive and glossy commercials with sexy voice-overs...

Well, it will make management feel better.

The ABC could run commercials but that would not permit Bob's mates to have a great deal of public money handed over to them, and that would be a shame because it's been an avowed policy of Bob's government to concentrate the media into the hands of this same group of mates.

The last resort would be to sell the ABC to the highest bidder. But there are no bidders. So get [the] bidder of last resort, Laurie Connell.

He'd see the potential – sell it to the buyer of last resort: the Western Australian government, and take a percentage on the way through.

Of course, Carmen then goes to Canberra, crying it was Peter's fault. Bob bails her out because he has to hold on to those seats in the West. Especially 'Rambo's' if he wants to keep the keys to the executive dunny.

And we all end up paying for a national broadcaster we just unloaded.

IT WAS CALLED the Wedding of the Year.

Some said the wedding of the decade.

And if Sir Robert Menzies was still with us, if he ever was, it would have been the 'I did but see them riding by...' wedding of the millennia.

I refer to once happily married Andrew, son of television's most famous family and Sarah, daughter of a pony-strangler from the Royal Catering Corps.

Amazing to me are the large number of people who have followed the couple's ups and downs in those bastions of journalistic integrity: *The Women's Weekly*, *The Woman's Day*, *New Idea* and *The Melbourne Truth* believing that it was the real thing.

This separation was, as is usual amongst celebrities, announced in the tabloids just before either party knows the divorce is coming.

It's accompanied with a photograph showing one party with a sixteen-year-old-part-time model and the other with a Texan oil millionaire.

People can't tell the difference between real life and the Royal family because everyone acts badly from time to time.

People are more than willing to pitch in with comments, criticisms and malicious gossip of their own to help the separation along.

So what if Fergie wore a paper bag on her head - how does that make the girl unfit to be a member of the Royal Family?

There are many members of the Royal Family that should have worn a paper bag on their heads - they'd have been a lot better off today, the Duke of Windsor for one.

Children must be considered in a separation - considered as valuable pawns in the nasty legal contest that is about to ensue.

The way to show a child attention is to launch a massive custody fight.

Andrew and Sarah were amazed at the reaction to the news that people actually thought they existed. There'll be a brief pre-divorce period, so as to allow the couple that popular, modern condition – no regrets. Having no regrets, as far as the fourth estate is concerned, is what robs royal scandals, and alcoholism, of poignancy.

But within a few short weeks it'll be back to who's up who, and who's paying the rent at Buckingham Palace.

The media hacks are absolutely right: who does Paul Keating think he is twisting the Royal tule and mentioning the 'R' word in front of them.

After all, the Royal Family belong to the fourth estate – they set them up, and they're going to knock them down.

LAST WEEK MY absence from the airwaves would have been noticed [and] open to interpretation.

Mick Malthouse, coach of the West Coast Eagles, invited me on a retreat with his players prior to the big game.

It's not widely known, Robert, that the West Coast Eagles are not just a bunch of guys with pituitary problems and tight shorts.

They're thinkers and in their thinking and their use of Australian Rules Football as a metaphor for existence, they are formidable!

When I spoke to them after a light training run, I began with Kierkegaard and Sartre, then returned to Spinoza, Kafka and Camus. You have observed, Robert, that in the heat and frenzy of the locker room, I abandoned chronological order.

I could see that Turley, Watters and McKenna were fascinated by my attack on morality, art, ethics, life and what to do with that last bit of soap on the rope.

Sumich said to me that a relation that relates itself to its own self must either have constituted itself, or have been constituted by another, but not on the full.

The concept brought tears to many of his team mates' eyes and this from a man who has trouble writing two meaningful sentences on 'My Day at the Zoo'.

True, the passage was totally incomprehensible but what of it, if Sumich was having fun? What a mind. What a surgical support.

Matera said that on the wing he found that the mind can never know his body, although it became friendly with his legs on a number of occasions.

Of course, Jakovich asked the question, during handball practice, which was, what can be said to be known, or to possess a knowness or knowability, or, at least, something you can mention to a teammate in the shower room?

As footballers, the West Coast Eagles understand that Cartesian dictum, 'I play footy, therefore I am', which might be better expressed [as] 'I didn't have a great impact on the game and I'll struggle when I'm asked to mind Brereton in the third quarter but I'll start the fourth quarter term on the interchange bench'.

The West Coast Eagles pose the problem: what can we actually know?

It's hard enough finding your way around Waverley looking for a hot dog. But, nevertheless, the West Coast Eagles have come to represent a body of philosophical work which I assure you, Robert, will have a place of reverence among the weightiest of thinkers.

Like Who? Like Hawthorn who creamed them on Saturday.

NOW I'D LIKE TO have a word or two or three with you, Robert, about precisely where we – that is, John Hewson and I – stand on the question where we stand with relation to the stance we're taking on the media beat-up regarding John's unfortunate circumstance.

And here, Robert, John and I are united in this – John and I.

Now, I've spoken about the invasion of one's privacy before. But John and I have had our heads together and got something straight between us.

And now what [will] you in the Fourth Estate will make of that!

I appreciate there is a body of opinion amongst the media hacks that John and his ex-wife only communicate through their seconds, but it's not true.

It's a concerted campaign to drive a gap the width of a Ferrari up the middle of the Liberal Party's support for John, that would allow Bob and his Visigoths to get home at another election.

John Hewson is an excellent leader, He's a man of immense parliamentary experience. He's an academic of some note from an American 'put your money in here, take your degree from the slot' university. And he's prepared to make the hard decisions.

How else could he have decided to leave his wife and kids two days before Christmas?

I respect this, the Liberal Party respects this, and I think everyone else ought to respect this too.

So what if his ex-wife has been reduced to hawking herself and the kids in *Sixty Minutes* for $50,000?

Where do you think she got that economic skill?

John could have the same influence on the rest of the nation as prime minister.

Just imagine a deregulated Australia, where labour costs will give Bangladesh a run for its money.

Why, just like the ex-Mrs Hewson, [we'll] will take the best offer that comes along.

JOHN KERIN HAS inextricably linked in [his] political career with his job as treasurer.

On top of John's quite staggering political acumen, there is a strong bond between him and the Prime Minister. John has the Prime Minister right behind him...

But, Sir Bruce, John Kerin's been sacked.

As I was about to say, Robert, you've got to be right behind someone if you want to stab them in the back.

Now, what was I talking about?

That's right. Ralph Willis has linked his political career with his job as Treasurer.

On top of Ralph's quite staggering political acumen, there is a strong bond between him and the Prime Minister.

Our listeners know this is all rubbish, don't they?

The only way Bob Hawke and the Labor Caucus can get together these days in the same room is with an approved counsellor in marriage guidance.

Bob's already explained the position as he sees the parts that suit him.

But you've got to understand how the Labor Party works.

Bob's a man of considerable accomplishment. He has brilliantly held the safe seat of Wills for the party.

His achievements in industrial relations are without peer: wages breakout of the '70s, oversaw reductions in real wages as the share market boomed, and the highest unemployment figures since the Great Depression.

After all, this is a democracy and Bob Hawke leads the party that made the man most people thought should have been the prime minster the country's governor-general.

QANTAS HAS CUT the pay for one hundred and thirty executives in a cost-cutting campaign to curb losses.

Now you might ask how these losses occurred.

Fifty million dollar losses, I might add. That's enough to run the ABC.

You could say it's the global recession. Or the Gulf War. Or even Peter's fault. But you'd be wrong.

QANTAS has come a 'gutsa' because of the deregulated competition of Rottnest Island Film Commission airlines.

Rottnest Island Film Commission Airlines, under the captaincy of Irving Flapp, former test pilot for Futility Aircraft, has boldly struck out where no corporate fat-cat or Humphrey Bear was prepared to go and take his superannuation.

Irving ordered an extra [plane], a third [plane], an assorted secondhand Mirage, and [a] F1-11A from our warrior leader, my friend Bob Hawke.

Since our victories in the Gulf, our enemies are convinced we've hold of guns to shoot, boats that float, and planes that fly.

The benefits for our travel industry and defence status are obvious.

We've got a plane that isn't going to crash inside the country. It proves to those overseas we mean business. And we don't have to take landing instructions from anyone we don't want to.

Now, I appreciate the two planes mentioned have been under a bit of a cloud. But with the fuselage chock-a-block with passengers, it won't be too long before [they?] locate problems and iron them out.

Mind you, some of our aircraft ironed themselves out comprehensively.

Our home maintenance problem has also cut costs dramatically; last person off washes it.

And passengers have to carry their own luggage off the plane.

[THERE IS A] possibility that, under certain circumstances – that is, the electorate having a gut-full and slinging Paul into opposition – he might consider the proposition of becoming a diplomat.

Of course, I'm not suggesting that Paul's not happy running the recession that brings home to bacon to the Banana Republic.

In fact, he's excellent at it.

Better than John Hewson [who] wants to add a tax to it.

Now, in the past weeks, Paul has impressed with his ability to make the decidedly cool statement, able to take the context of a joint communique and confirm our mutual respect while reaffirming our meaningful relationship with the neighbourhood bully, I mean, regional stabilizer.

Paul's qualifications to be a diplomat are comprehensive, which is about as far as his schooling went.

His linguistic ability; you need half-a-dozen Italian dialects if you're going to deal with the New South Wales right.

In Indonesia, Paul, when dealing with the thorny question of human rights, demonstrated a facility to say nothing at all in several different ways in English.

At several press conferences, Paul amazed us all, and even his hosts, by being trapped by the Fourth Estate into saying anything other than nothing at all.

The only way we spotted the difference was when Paul's language changed when he spoke to Melanesians as opposed to Indonesians.

He told the Papua-New Guinea government to lift its game on law-and-order, and [on] human rights abuses, otherwise the aid deals are off. He doesn't get pushed around.

What a diplomat! Paul isn't pushed around on regional affairs...

WITH THE RAPID movement of several indices, I know some dentists who have become the equivalent of Hong Kong commodity dealers.

So for the first time in a lot of people's lives, their heads have become the most useful section of their person.

If you're going to [be?] a broker, then there [are] a few facts of life – economic ones.

It depends on whether you can check the market, diminish returns by off-setting the saving and investment reference while depreciating an internal devaluation of disposable savings in the short term gain over the rate that foreign investment liquidity in the June quarter – take away the number you first thought of.

In simple terms: get an expensive suit, car, woman, business assistant and cellular phone – money [will be] needed to maintain these.

The *big* money is the *new* money and the *new* money is Arab money. The American dollar isn't holding its value, and the Deutschmark is going to [*indecipherable*] up.

Buy things that hold their value: Filipino brides, Korean children, and Queensland politicians.

But don't let that word 'economics' scare the c... pants off you, because no matter what happens to interest rates, unemployment, a flat-tax rate or the scientific possibility of lancing the cat's boils under water, as a broker you're always spending someone else's money.

And that means you can keep the suit, car, woman, business associates and cellular phone.

PAUL'S BIG ECONOMIC Statement is an attempt by a prime minister who is as popular as genital warts to dress up the economy for an electoral outing.

The kids are in the back seat, right behind Paul – if I can continue the metaphor – and the chassis has been stripped back and redesigned. The only trouble is the 'donk' dropped out on the driveway.

I'm here as Paul's last minute probe.

The last incumbent of the Lodge let me sit on his right hand; Paul insists I sit on his lap.

You, Broadfield, and our respected listeners are going to shape our nation's destiny.

Paul wants us to make people understand what he is trying to do.

Paul's tired of being the fellow who gets to stand around sticking his finger in and out of the dyke of economic disaster. When will the people realise that he's the Prime Minister, not the Treasurer?

It's John Dawkin's turn to wander about the country being grumpy – or any of the other dwarfs.

Paul said to me, 'Running the country is not like running a home.'

In fact, I'm thinking of letting the Labor Party run my home.

This recession is the one that Paul inherited from the out-going Prime Minister...

As Paul said: the glories that were the Napoleonic Empire Clock factory weren't built in the post-war period with a three-year gap for Whitlam's progressive radical policies.

Essentially, Paul's already announced his vision. He did when he was Treasurer all those years ago when he brought home the bacon to balance out the diet of coconuts.

People have to work hard and stop asking for more money or better conditions.

Paul can't look after everyone. He's already got a list of those he's been looking after, and he'd like you to know that the wife and kids appreciate the heated swimming pool at the Lodge.

AS SUBSCRIBERS TO the German magazine *Stern* are aware, they are going to be made party to the horrid diaries of the ABC Radio Love God.

In Broadfield's case, writing is a highly recommended form of leisure activity.

It takes up large amounts of time if, like, Rob, you haven't mastered running writing, and if you really think a great deal of yourself.

Now, as people know I'm not one to stick my nose or any other part of my anatomy in anyone else's business.

But even with a cursory glance at the Broadfield Diaries, I couldn't put Rob's business down.

And once you have [I had?] got it in your [my?] hands, between your [my?] fingers, it convinced me that they were written with a heap of business in mind; you can smell the potential.

As an author, Rob hadn't let the fact that his life hasn't been as fascinating as it might have been stop him.

Rob simply made it all up.

Rob mentions his travels. Venice, where he stripped off all his gear and swam everywhere: The Doggie's Palace, and how he wrote to the RSPCA, saying how well the Italians looked after their animals.

The Broadfield Diaries also reveal an iconoclast. Quite often he states how unimpressed he was with the Pyramids, Eiffel Tower, London, New York and every major piece of European art since 1643.

He's never actually seen them but, like many of us, he's seen pictures of them and [tells] us what he thought.

Of course, the excerpts of the Broadfield Diaries are handsomely illustrated with photographs of the rich and famous with Rob's picture stuck on.

But they represent in their publication an opportunity to understand what a wonderful person Rob Broadfield is and how he's been consistently misunderstood by his friends, mentors, everyone who ever met him and most of the riff-raff who created European art since 1643.

IT'S OUR DAUGHTER Anthea's birthday this week.

Lady Fernargle-Jones and myself were sitting on the rubberised sheeting of her bed just as she left it twelve long months ago.

She's not dead; she's gone to Tassie.

Rambo Beazley called and Anthea went off to support Australia's actions in the Gulf War by seeing active service in Tasmania for the Defence Department.

Since there, we've heard little snippets of her new life. We were going to put her photograph on the back of a taxi but very few taxi companies use prime-movers.

She joined the Snugglepot/Cuddlepie/Painters-and-Dockers Revolution – any Marxist-Leninist Drama Laboratory where she got rave reviews for taking some [of] Andrew Lloyd Webber's most relevant and committed musicals to Central Australia and staging them at all the top Aboriginal gigs.

There's a crying need for a permanent Lloyd Webber theatre for Aborigines, like they've got in North Korea.

My daughter recognises that there are still large sections of the Australian black community who have never heard a bar of Andrew Lloyd Webber's subversive avant-garde theatre.

Anthea has now carved a career in radio. She a free-wheeling, socio-aesthetic, non-linear, hyper-responsive presenter on the ABC.

She's brought to Tasmanian Bakelite a break, a hang-up free, kick-out-the-urban-elitism, step-over toehold little ratings winner: She's been presenting the hog futures and apple weather alerts.

Socially, she's hit Hobart social life, seen at the best spots, hanging out at the Battery Point Maritime Blue Light Disco.

Anthea moves with the fast crowd in Main Road.

We heard that she got mixed up with drugs.

I'm not a wowser – non-brand cigarettes [?] – coke [?]

She's been dropping LBDs – little black dresses.

Imagine how shocked we were when we heard of Anthea dancing naked at midnight down at Port Arthur, the former penal colony.

With her native Western Australia lacking in convict heritage, her doctor has advised that she may be suffering from Penal Envy.

A MATTER OF the very gravest consequences, and I'm not fooling about here.

I want to plonk it on the table before the listening public of this great nation of ours, steeped, as it were, in a military tradition – fourteen wars in less than a century – to get a feeling for what has happened internationally.

There has been a suggestion in the media that the full story of the Kuwait stand-off has yet to be told.

There's always some moron claiming we've got to be in the area. (*Sir Bruce. ? Robert Broadfield*)

I don't know who the maniac is and I don't care really. (*Sir Bruce. ? Robert Broadfield*)

But there is always a fringe element prepared to abandon reason, rabble-rousing a decent society and getting maudlin over some lines drawn on a map by an office johnny in London in the 1920s. (*Sir Bruce. ? Robert Broadfield*)

According to this ratbag we're going, on a date suggested by us, to drop in with a punitive force amounting to the biggest surprise anyone's seen since December 7th 1941. (*Sir Bruce, Hawke supports this. ? Robert Broadfield.*)

Well, on the other hand, I see where this all makes a lot of sense.

Now the gaff's been blown, I suppose I can reveal where the wheels came off the diplomatic cart.

I was contacted by a long-standing acquaintance of mine from the CIA, Crypto T. Fascist.

Now Crypto and I go back many years. For a long time, he was based in Australia.

We went scuba-diving in the 1960s, off Portsea Beach as a matter of fact.

We'd hang around the Hilton Hotel in Sydney, and he gave me a guided tour of Yarralumla in the mid-'70s.

I digress. Anyway, Crypto suggested I have another chat to Saddam before the top secret date.

So I invited Saddam and his lovely wife Beryl to spend New Year with us in Western Australia's magnificent wine-growing region of Margaret River while I tried to persuade him that George and the guys intended using live ammunition in and around the opening in his Bombay Bloomers.

We waited and waited – no Saddam, no Beryl, no phone call. So I suppose he's getting Beryl and the girls to dig away from the exploding ironmongery headed his way.

I realised, finally, how seriously Saddam takes this Islam stuff that he wouldn't risk personal injury to life and limb to taste a few vintages.

Funny lot, aren't they?

MANY OF OUR listeners would be waiting to hear about what really went on at the stripped-to-the-bone Premiers' Conference.

Which side was Sir Bruce going to be on?

But the premiers made it easy for this old fence-sitter.

They came with their wish list, ready to sit on Santa Keating's knee.

It seems that everyone in the country has got the idea that the cupboard is bare – except the premiers.

So I wrote out the estimates with a big crayon and dangled them over their heads from balloons and light aircraft.

This seemed to get their attention and a few got an inkling about what's going on.

That is, Paul as prime minister and former treasurer is tired of standing around sticking his finger in the dyke of the premiers' bad economic decisions.

Of course, the former incumbent of the Lodge wasn't averse to fingering the dyke his rich mates punctured from time to time, but those days are over.

Of course, there are elements of the way things are going that would disturb anyone: the collapse of Medicare, the youth unemployment rate, and how soon Paul can shoehorn Richo back into the ministry.

Well, some of the States at any rate – Victoria – we might have to sell off for pig feed.

Paul let the Premiers know that he's got his priorities. In fact, he's got a list of them somewhere but he can't remember what he did with it.

The Premiers may have it, but they refuse to take treatment for it – just more money.

Where would we be without premiers or State governments or the attendant bureaucratic duplications?

Now, there's an idea!

JEFF KENNETT, WITH my guidance, produced a finely tuned state-of-the-art industrial relations policy.

Basically it is a warning. And Jeff is presenting his warning of the power of the unions by an enormous increase in the number of strikes Victorians will be presented with.

Jeff has wasted no time in taking on those militant unions who have brazenly maintained the wages accord hammered out with those socialists in Canberra.

The same radical Stalinist fellow-travellers who have seen a real reduction in wages over ten years that has, in effect, crushed personal freedom and given Australia the lowest inflation rate in thirty years. Chaos!

Kennett will, with my guiding hand, be an inspiration to others.

He'll have the Western Hemisphere gasping at his audacity.

And that's not bad given that Britain is the current title holder and natural home of industrial chaos.

Industrial disputes don't just happen. They're caused. And this just where the whole Kearner government wimped out.

Who cares if the trains run on time, or at all?

Or whether babies have milk or cows, for that matter.

Jeff is committed, or at least he should be!

And to prove I'm behind him, I'm going to take a pay increase of fifty percent.

I'D LIKE TO draw people's attention to Christmas.

Christmas is the thing that interrupts the usual murder and mayhem that passes for the civilised world at this time of year.

Most people have, in the clamour of the Yuletide rattle of cash registers, forgotten the significance of Christmas.

Most have [so] forgotten by about Christmas party number two, three days before the final kick-off, that the whole thing goes over their scones.

Just before you sit down to knock over your twenty-nine course nibbles:

* Rise above the obvious shortcomings of your family;
* Put aside your distaste [of] or discomfort with the people they married and diluted the family gene pool with;
* Think of those who have given so [you] may enjoy Christmas – the retailers, keeping their shops open in these hardened economic times;
* Think of the TV stars who leave their families in the middle of August to record a mind-rotting Christmas Special.

Have a good Christmas and I hope you lose your car keys.

OF COURSE, IT has now come to everyone's attention that it is all over between them. [*who?* – editor]

Quite often I find myself taken aside and forced to give advice to young people on the nature of relationships.

They say to me, is it better to be the lover or the loved one?

Of course, neither, if your cholesterol is over 600.

I'm talking about romantic love. The love between a man and a woman, rather than between a mother and child, or a child and their pet, or a lawyer and his Porsche, or two airline attendants.

To be loved is different from being admired but, as I say, to really love someone it is essential to be in the same room with the person.

You have to be a good lover. You must be strong. I suppose being able to lift a few kilos should do it.

The loved one must be the most beautiful thing in the world even though to a stranger they may look like a vegetarian stick insect.

Because love is blind and it helps if it is a little deaf and dumb too.

The joys of love sound like a hit song. It's a pity that it's too close to 'Highway to Hell'.

IT APPEARS AS, given the course of their recent debates, that the presidency, up until now left pretty much in the hands of central casting, is about to be taken over.

Not by the Lone Ranger, Tonto or even, as in recent years, by the threat of Trigger [Silver?], given that Tonto has a dicky ticker and a propensity to redecorate other dignitary's suits.

The lead role in the next episode of the American Dream seems to be landing in the lap of an old pacifist protest buddy, Bill Clinton.

And I notice that Bill, against a minefield of cavilling and mud-slinging, says he will do the job to the best of his ability.

Now, if that's not a get-out clause then I'll go 'ee-aw'.

Of course, Bill doesn't have the experience of the Great Renaldo, world's first semi-retired US President and Sheriff of Dodge for an hour-and-a-half in 1948 for seventy minutes.

But his knowledge is impressive and aside from anything else, if he can avoid becoming a splat [sic] on the landscape in South East Asia, then he's [sic] must have a few outs for the New World Order.

I SUPPOSE MANY of you sense a wave of very genuine relief at the recent announcement from the prefect's room in Canberra.

Gay people would no longer [be] stuffed into 65mm calibre howitzers and fired over the horizon.

This, of course, presupposes that the collective military had a human rights policy [in] comparison with their intended purpose, which is a lack of human rights through killing, maiming and mutilating people who aren't us.

Human rights are a baffle to even the most beaten eye.

Because we know that non-friendly nations are no respecters of human rights, which allows us to classify them as 'one of them'.

Then it follows, why would we, hypothetically, assume the 'one of them' wants to point [the] business end of a taxpayer-provided weapon at 'one of them'.

I mean – it flies in the face of nature: 'one of them' shooting at 'one of them'.

Remember, there's the right way to do it and the military way to do it!

BEFORE FIELDING ANY questions from you, Robert, on today's events in Victoria, I'd just like to make a couple of points about industrial relations Jeff Kennett-style.

We've had someone's work cut out trying to describe Jeff's policy but that's all for the good of Victoria.

So, obviously, I can't explain Jeff's policy.

As you can see, Jeff requires no fancy footwork in the finely-tuned line of warning people about the enormous number of strikes.

Jeff's going to prove his ability to manage the nation's production lines even if, or especially if, they're not producing.

But Jeff's not unsympathetic. He has made it abundantly clear that standard stoppages are alright – for tea, lunch and compassionate leave like the death of the pit pony or one of the kids has got stuck up a chimney.

Jeff is a breath of nineteenth-century laissez-faire capitalism. I might even down tools and demand something.

I WANT EVERYONE to understand this: Australia is going to have pay television.

I know that it's considered strange for a Prime Minister to decide to have pay TV and then have an enquiry about whether or not we're going to have it.

But that's how Paul's mind works.

You introduce pay TV; it immediately puts the opposition on the back foot because Bob Menzies didn't leave any policies on that before he checked out.

And it gets the media off the scent of the opinion polls.

Then you have an enquiry into whether or not we've already got pay TV.

It's simple!

Of course, pay TV is going to force a re-evaluation of the industry as a whole, and this is where the Rottnest Island Film Commission comes in.

I've established, by depositing a small, non-refundable government grant in the central bank of the Marshall Islands and using a letter of reference and a business contact given to me by Richo, the Rottnest Island Film Commission Television Centre.

I'm hoping, once granted the licence, that, like all other Australian television entrepreneurs, this will really pay off and we'll lose a lot of money.

Hard work is the important thing. Hard work and a lot of other people's money. And some gin.

And a luxury yacht with room for the polo ponies and guest rooms for old mates out on day release.

Of course, after I've done with that holding operation for a while, we then pass it onto the only blokes who wanted it in the first place: Rupert Murdoch or Kerry Packer.

Oh, the left wing of the ALP wouldn't have put up with that.

[THE CONCEPT OF] Forward Defence has become: 'keeping them off the rose bushes next to the swans in the front garden'.

The government should hang warning signs that stipulate where or what parts of the nation are likely to become recreational battlefields in the event of invasion.

Remember: projectiles can hurt.

The general public would be well advised not to holiday in adjacent vicinities.

A ballistic incursion, as we call it, can spoil even the best-planned holiday.

Unexploded ammunition shouldn't be handled, stoked or fondled in any way.

Now, as we know, there is *no* chance that these lethal bits of ironmongery are likely to land outside the prescribed area. That's what my contacts in the military assure me. *And* they wouldn't lie [just] because we're at war!

I think people would take comfort just knowing that their holiday or even their home is of military importance.

Names like Vaucluse, Dalkeith [and] Toorak could be a warning to our enemies – just in case their military intelligence hasn't given them the full picture.

Massed rage, driven by wealthy, blue-rinsed matrons is a force to be reckoned with.

While their sons are defending us in 'front line' Tasmania.

TELECOMMUNICATIONS.

Kim-Sat, [an initiative of] 'Rambo' [Beazley], allows the Rottnest Island Film Commission to vertically branch out into television.

Australians can have the benefit of Sir Bruce over their heads, beaming down straight into their faces.

On the Rottnest Island Film Commission, we'll have no repeats. There'll be no *schlock* fillers when the boys from McNair Anderson aren't offering potential viewers steak knives as prizes.

News will be anchored by either Fat Cat or Humphrey Bear because parents have difficulty getting kids to watch quality TV like news.

[There will be] more quality from Quokka-Sat via Kim-Sat. [We have] bought up a lot of top-notch Iraqi television.

We've got *Saddam Hussein: Portrait of a Genius and Short-order Chef.* This is a doco on a humble hotel doorman in a fancy uniform who grew up to be a fanatic in a fancy uniform.

Then that great Iraqi mini-series *The True Believers* starts. Jack Thompson and Jackie Weaver do impersonations of great Muslim politicians going way back to the rise of Saddam Hussein.

We were going to have Geoffrey Robertson do a 'Hypothetical' but he asked Saddam Hussein the wrong question and parts of Geoffrey went missing suddenly.

Margaret Fulton will be hosting *Fundamentalist Cooking with Nerve Gas.* She'll be demonstrating (by beating her chest) how to cook and prepare what remains of Geoffrey Robertson.

[All] that's starting now. [It only needs] a budget aerial – free from [any] dry cleaner.

NOT EVERYONE CAN be a pilot or a doctor – for economic reasons mainly.

You can't be a pilot because Bob Hawke wants to deregulate Sir Peter's airline.

Peter didn't want to. Bob had to offer him a lot of tax-payers money.

Then Bob thought he could help by flogging the competition off to Sir Peter's mates down at the Stock Exchange.

Not true. Bob's going [to] float Australian Airlines. Ordinary Australians who earn on average $22,500 per annum are going to be beating a path to the Stock Exchange as they have to purchase on [for] the foreign exchange market – why else would the TV channels report [it] unless we were all involved? – like the great old days of 1929.

Unfortunately, as we know, not everyone can be a doctor in the metropolitan areas of Australia. There just isn't that amount of money to go around.

When city doctors talk about servicing we patients I can't help but recall my days on the Poll Hereford Board.

[There is] a problem with John Flynn's idea: no waiting room cluttered with malingering types with suspected strains of the left nostril.

[Nor are there] opportunities to [listen] to the tales of drunkards and the bone-idle while the meter runs.

John didn't even think to consider where his doctors and pilots could park the Volvo, practice their chip shots or anti-foul the yacht. And where's the Grange collection going to go.

And I was right. So John and his Flying Doctor Service need the cash.

You have a bingle in the Bush and see how long your local GP [takes to] treat that priority.

I HAVEN'T BEEN on Quok-Sat 1 at all.

You've been probing the fundamental orifice of truth and realised that there was more than sunshine emanating. It's no wonder, Robert, you're in the position that you're in. And I hope it gives you great pleasure.

This has been a smokescreen put up by ASIO.

They've achieved this by setting fire to Lionel Murphy's old file.

I was in Britain, counselling Margaret Thatcher.

I've known that woman (although not in the Biblical sense) man and boy for many years.

I see the Iron Lady when she's popped a few rivets and lets out a bit of water.

The names were what hurt: 'Attila the Hen' or 'Dirty Harriet'.

I recall Denis saying to me, 'Sir Bruce, there's a pub open over there, and I think it's open'.

Economically, she's transformed Britain. Since she was anti-Keynesian, she embraced Milton Friedman just as Chile did under Alan's mate Pinochet: 3 million [to] have employment opportunities building jails.

Given a few more years Margaret could have taken the UK back to its glorious past: kids up chimneys, ponies down mines, and old people in workhouses.

Margaret had a vision of the Chunnel, so six hundred people could travel from Birmingham to Paris every fifteen minutes.

But where were they going to find six hundred Parisians who'd want to go to Birmingham?

Don't let reality impinge.

"LOVECOD" AS AN ANKLEBITER

The only known work of art by Sir Bruce Fernargle-Jones outside the Louvre.
The enigmatic caption suggests this is a pen drawing of Robvert Broadfiled, the presenter of the
ABC radio programme that featured Sir Bruce.
The authenticity of the artwork is uncertain as it is not signed. The Curator of the National Gallery
of Australia, when consulted, replied, 'It could well be, but who cares?'

Although Sir Bruce Fernargle-Jones, in the broadcasts reproduced in the previous pages, occasionally avers to his more than occasionally addressing party conferences, conventions, and gatherings of other kinds (including possibly Country Women's Association meetings), there is little evidence – other than his own assertions – that he did so other than sporadically at best, and probably reluctantly even then, unless a fee was attached.

Reproduced below, however, are two speeches delivered by Sir Bruce. It is unclear as to the dates of these two addresses but it seems fairly clear the first was made before he was appointed Chairman of the Rottnest Island Film Commission and the second during his tenure in the sinecure. The second, by the context of its remarks, was made on or about July 28, 1981.

*

I

Good evening ladies and gentlemen - I'd like welcome each and every one of you especially one gentleman, I don't know where he's sitting but he retired today after 25 years as an assistant manager at Coles New World and to mark the occasion his associates presented him with a gold shopping trolley – isn't that nice? Everything about it was gold — the basket was gold, the handle was gold and the four wheels were gold. And just to make him feel really at home, three gold wheels move in one direction while the fourth moves in another.

You know I'm from the land, ladies and gentlemen, the country, that is. You know when a farmer puts a bull together with a cow it's known as the bull servicing the cow and now you know what government authorities mean when they say they've been servicing us for all these years.

Now I am interested in government authorities because I've been the sitting member for the state seat of Lower Wandering for the past – nigh on twenty years but Don Dunston, our premier, said, 'Bruce, why don't you try going to Canberra?' He said, 'A man of your obvious talents wouldn't do any harm to the Federal Labor Party's image...' I suppose what he means is Australia doesn't need a Lynch, it needs a Fernargle-Jones. So tonight, ladies and gentlemen I'd like to take my first step to those hallowed pig-iron halls by officially making my first Bill Hayden-approved speech.

Ladies and gentlemen, I feel the time has come for me to speak out – for I believe as many of us believe that we will – all of us as we have before and can, nay, must once again if we are to be – and make no mistake about it – we cannot afford not to be – for, and let us be perfectly clear about this – in the past few months we have proved without any shadow of doubt, that we do – and will continue to do, strongly, firmly and gently as we have in the past and we are quite capable of doing yet again – need I say more? But! And this is a big but – now at the same time and this is a decision only you can make – shall we?

Looking forward as we do – as we all do, indeed as it is our duty to do at this hour of decision – or not, that is the question you must ask yourselves tonight – but I hear you saying, 'Ah! If it were only that clear!' Now I know, and here I must disagree for a moment, for where would this country be but for this great land of ours? – and I have the facts to bear me out. Today in this country 30% - or to put it another way, thirty in every hundred, or to put it in simple terms 6.7 in every 22.4 as compared to 3% of the entire population for the previous four years. What other party can make that claim?

But we can't do it alone. We believe as we've always believed and will always believe, for without the future there can be no tomorrow. Should we go on supporting foreign dictators or take better care of the ones we have at home? It is essential at this moment, when our beloved country has its back to the wall that we realise how exciting that can be. For only with one's back to the wall can one go forward – forward to the next wall. No, I believe that we and when I say we, I mean us, all of us, strong in our weakness but weak in our strength, never fleeing from fear but never fearing to flee, can so strive to preserve, nay, strengthen the pillars of apathy and inequality that we have laboured so long to build.

And prove to the world there are bigger, better greater crisis ahead.

Goodnight and God bless me! And remember, if you've got half a mind to go into politics that's all you need and as voters you are particularly precious to me, so on the way home remember to take care because nine out of ten people are caused by accidents.

Thank you, thank you, thank you, Roy, for those warm words. Words are inadequate to express the sort of feeling I get in the pit of my stomach for you, Roy. Roy and I go way back together, but I wish Roy would go back even further because I think he trod on something nasty on the way here tonight.

And talking about something nasty, I would like to address myself to the reason we are all hear tonight. That is, of course, the royal weeding between Prince Charles and Lady Di.

Since being elevated to the heights of knighthoodship for my services to maintaining Australia's image abroad, that is, by telling lies through the medium of the cinematograph, I have had occasion to observe the workings of the nobility at first hand.

Take for example Princess Anne. You too would drive fast if you had been brought up travelling everywhere with your mum at fifteen miles per hour. No wonder they always wave frantically everywhere they go.

I travel extensively world-wide, but I always come back to Australia because I believe that a man needs to keep close contact with his roots.

And I understand that Prince Charles fondness for travelling on British Rail indicates that he shares the same point of view.

I had the extreme pleasure and honour of meeting the Prince of Wales at a Royal Garden Party last summer when I was in London for the Cannes Film Festival. I didn't see too many films but I did manage to brown nose my way into the Garden Party at Buckingham Palace. While I was sucking on an Edwardian cucumber sandwich, His Royal Highness approached me. With a regal gesture, he pressed a used teabag into my hand and said, 'Dispose of this, my good man'. Remembering at that crucial moment, the advice of my good friend, Roy Cleghorn, I quickly thrust it up a passing Corgi.

I also further cemented my relationship with the royal family when I was able to assist her Majesty by loaning her a crowbar, I happened to have with me to enable her to get Prince Andrew off one of the guests.

Princess Anne entertained us with her impressions of famous stars of screen, stage and television. Namely, Trigger, Fury, National Velvet and Mr Ed. Her husband, Captain Mark Phillips then joined his wife for a riding exhibition.

So tonight I feel like I have had a big one thrust into my lap. Namely the honour of proposing a toast to the future Mr and Mrs Windsor, or as they are, know to their friends and enemies alike, as Noddy and Bigears.

As my good lady wife, Lady Doris, is in London at this very moment attending the Los Angeles Film Festival for tax purposes, she has been honoured to be amongst the lucky recipients of an invitation to stand in the Mall, rain or shine, and watch the procession go past. When I spoke to her on the phone just before I came here tonight, Lady Doris told me how wonderful it was that all our Commonwealth brethren were making preparations of their own for the happy occasion – especially the Irish who were all gathering to try to ensure them a big send-off.

So on behalf of everyone here tonight I have taken the liberty of sending the following telegram at your expense to the royal couple: TO THE PRINCE AND PRINCESS OF WALES. I KNOW WHAT YOU ARE DOING IN LONDON TONIGHT. STOP. I HOPE, SIR, THAT YOU CAN DO FOR LADY DI WHAT MRS THATCHER IS DOING FOR THE COUNTRY, and I signed it: YOURS TILL THE COWS COME HOME TO ROOST, SIR BRUCE FERNARGLE-JONES, ROY CLEGHORN AND TWO HUNDRED DRUNKEN LOUTS. PS THANK YOU MOTHER FOR THE RABBITS.

So I would ask you all to charge your glasses to the company expense account, and to be upstanding, those of you who are still able to walk, or not too pissed to at least stagger to your own two feet, while I give you Prince Charles and Lady Di, and you're welcome to them.

AN UNEXPECTED INTRUSION OF ANOTHER VOICE.

It seems that at the peak of his self-assumed popularity, Sir Bruce, in an uncharacteristic display of personal generosity, extended an invitation to Roy Cleghorn, one-time fellow board member of the Rottnest Island Film Commission, to occasionally contribute to his programme. (See Part 2 for a further explanation of Roy Cleghorn and his place in the Rottnest Island Film Commission story.)

At the time Cleghorn was in the United States of America. It is not clear why, as his ASIO file has been embargoed indefinitely. Apparently, it was felt by Sir Bruce that Cleghorn may be inveigled into offering an occasional comment on the state of the States, to perhaps round-out Sir Bruce's far more wide-ranging and insightful purview of matters local, national and international.

Cleghorn appears to have accepted the invitation. However, rather more characteristically, Sir Bruce completely forgot about having extended it.

The following transcript was found among the Fernargle-Jones papers, so it seems that Cleghorn attempted a first (and only) 'Message Stick from America with Roy Cleghorn'.

The editor feels ill-equipped to comment on whether the airwaves would have been impoverished by the Cleghorn contribution or whether the radio firmament was enriched by the absence of this and/or any subsequent material.

A MESSAGE STICK FROM AMERICA WITH ROY CLEGHORN

You know I was having a bit of a chinwag with my old mate Alistair Cooke the other arvo. Cookie had heard on the bush telegraph that I was going to be doing for the mob back in Oz what he has been slipping to the Poms for about a hundred years give or take the odd decade. Anyway, ever since little Enzie Macaroni invented the steam wireless, my old mate Cookie has been giving the Poms the low-down on doings here in the land of the Septic Tanks, and since he figures he is a sort of dowager to giving-the-good-oilers hereabouts, who am I to deflate the boring old windbag. Besides, it was his shout.

Well, Old Cookie had it on his tiny mind to give me the drum on what a century or two bending the ears of the long-suffering Pommie public had taught him about the Yanks. I'm not a bloke to pass up a free pointer or two even if they probably aren't worth a pinch of the proverbial nanny goat's – which they're mostly not once Cookies had a couple.

This time Cookie came up with the goods. 'Roy old china', he says to me, 'If you want to get the drop on the Americans, all you got to do is etch in your noggin this simple truth: Yanks figure they can do anything'. And, you know, Cookie for once in his life hit the bull right on the horns.

That's just what the Yanks reckon they can do – anything they bloody want to. Now I'm not talking here about them flogging off to some tiny god-forsaken spit-drop of a country and beating the crap out of the local peasants just because the boss-cockie has been turning a few quid slipping the odd pharmaceutical product over the border. And then putting the wind up the local nuns and bishops and what-all by blasting Heavy Metallic Rocks at them out of their tanks. Course the Yanks can do all that – and they did! But that's routine stuff for them!

Your intrepid investigator Roy has sniffed out more disturbing bits of dope – if you'll pardon the pun. In addition to the Yanks interfering with Third World peasants, they are interfering with nature as well. What these blokes are up to now is: dentistry for doggies.

Yeah. Now, if an American pooch snaps off a canine or three munching on the postie's shins, the mugs that own it, provided the postie hasn't blown said pooch away to doggie heaven with a Magnum 44 as happen here not so long ago, then the owners can pop around to their nearest doggie dentist and have a set of false gnashers whacked in its gob

If some doting owner doesn't like little Fido's bite – I don't mean how big a chunk it can take out of the neighbours but its over-bite, say – a few thousand bucks of dentistry and Fido has a set of pearly whites the envy of all the mutts in the street.

And you can now buy special breath freshening doggie tucker to keep the little cur from killing you with the pong of lingering Chum.

But, as you know, I never take anything at face value, not even a dog with breath as fresh as a mountain spring even if it has got bits of the postie's strides hanging out of it slavering chops. There is more to this than meets the eye or the gums in this case.

What I figure is that if Yankee dentists can stick teeth into animals' cake holes, they can take them out too. And this is what I reckon is really going on. The Yanks are sick and tired of their citizens becoming din-dins for the indigenous wildlife when they pop down to Oz for a bit of a break at me old mate Hoge's invitation. So don't be surprised if there is a big leap in the number of Yank dentists and vets dropping in on Oz for a holiday. And an outbreak of reports of unwary tourists getting their appendages sucked by gummy crocs.

Still, some good could come of it. A lot of babies will sleep easier on camping trips into the great outback if dingo dentistry takes off down under.

Oo-roo till next time.

PART II

THE ROTTNEST ISLAND FILM COMMISSION – THE GENESIS THEREOF TOGETHER WITH THE PART PLAYED THEREIN BY SIR BRUCE FERNARGLE-JONES AND HIS RESURRECTION

The Rottnest Island Film Commission originated as a simple, throw-away, one-line joke by Bill Lyon sometime around 1979 or 1980. (The actual date of this momentous occasion went unrecorded, as it was not seen as being potentially or actually a momentous occasion.) For reasons best known to himself, Lyon expounded this joke to Neil Rattigan, together with his feeling that it could perhaps, suitably expanded, be used as the basis of a series of sketches for radio. (Five-minute comedy sketches were prevalent on radio in those days.)

Rattigan, for reasons best kept to himself, was sufficiently either (a) amused or (b) intrigued to agree the idea (if it can be so dignified) had some merit. He agreed to collaborate with Lyon on extending the concept into fully realised (in their own minds) radio sketch material. (Others, as will be seen below, were less convinced of the notion of 'fully realised'.) A number of scripts which eventuated from this collaborate are reproduced in these pages shortly.

Sir Bruce Fernargle-Jones was the first character Lyon and Rattigan created on the way to 'populating' the sketches and, of course, the Rottnest Island Film Commission itself. It was clear that the Commission would require a chairman (this was still an acceptable designation at the time) and so Sir Bruce was born. A few more details as to who (or what) he was are given below in sections relating to the main characters who came, in time, to sit upon the Board of the Rottnest Island Film Commission or were employees thereof.

In short, however, other than for Sir Bruce, the Board came to consist of Rex ('Slick') Piranha, pre-owned car salesman, Roy Cleghorn, TV naturalist (and pre-curser by several decades of 'Russell Coight') with other, casual members, not all of whom came to fruition in the limited number of scripts that were actually written.

These included Wayne Bertolucci, Arthur Director, Ramita and Jamita (neither of whom were graced with surnames), and Nosmo King. The employees of the Commission who were created in the writing process were Mervyn Whipple, the administrative assistant, and Dolly Mixture, Sir Bruce's personal assistant. Bert, an ancient janitor, came with the (fictional) premises – an abandoned below-ground-level public convenience.

As the concept transmogrified from radio sketches to a television series (perforce, because nobody wanted the radio version), some of these characters 'disappeared' and others were added, notably Arlene Farquhar, a television news presenter who was frequently called upon to offer commentary on events surrounding the Rottnest Island Film Commission. One-off characters also abounded, depending on the story demands of the radio or television scripts.

As will be – regrettably – noted in the pages that follow the Lords of Radio and Television in this country (and at least one other) declined to be dazzled by the humour, wit, comic invention, and/or commercial potential of the Rottnest Island Film Commission, and Lyon and Rattigan moved on to other projects. With one noticeable exception.

A decade or so after Sir Bruce Fernargle-Jones (and the Rottnest Island Film Commission to which, as has been seen previously, he frequently referred) was brought back to life (or, if that is a trifle too metaphysical) back into fictional existence as the persona adopted by Lyon for the comic commentaries recorded in Part 1. These were entirely the work of Lyon himself (although just occasionally making use of aspects of Sir Bruce and the Rottnest Island Film Commission from those dear, dark days and dear, dark scripts gone by). Sir Bruce and the Rottnest Island Film Commission has become inextricably linked in Lyon's impersonation. The pages that follow may give some further indication of where Sir Bruce came from. But probably not why. Some things in the Cosmos we inhabit must remain without explication– Professor Brian Cox notwithstanding.

WHY ROTTNEST ISLAND?

The existential ramifications of attempting to answer this question (or even to ask it in the first place) are too great to be dealt with here. And are probably irrelevant anyway.

More to the point (if there is one) is why 'Rottnest Island' was chosen by Bill Lyon as the core of the joke – satire, if you will – at the expense of the (then) obsession with film commissions, corporations, bodies, etc which were springing up, like mythical dragon's teeth (albeit armed only with government funds) seemingly all over the Australia.

To Western Australians, such as Lyon and Rattigan, Rottnest Island was the most unlikely place to have a film commission and yet sufficiently well-known to give the joke some resonance.

Be this as it may (or may not), there might be poor benighted souls who are not Western Australian or even come from there perusing this humble volume to whom Rottnest Island is an obscure reference too far. Of course, such pitiful individuals might take recourse to the Internet and become better informed – perhaps.

But to place Lyon's and Rattigan's recourse to the idea of a film commission on (or allegedly situated on) Rottnest Island in context, it is useful at the conjuncture to reflect upon what Rottnest Island was in the late 1970s when they made merriment with the notion. This requires a brief historical detour.

Rottnest Island, a speck of limestone and sand dunes, some 18 kilometres off the coast had been there (as an island that is) for about 7,000 years*. For most that time, and probably well before it, it had been the haunt of venomous snakes, the lizards that tried to avoid being dinner for the same, sundry birds (usually transitory), seals and, most importantly, quokkas.

Quokkas are diminutive marsupials rather like wallabies that have shrunk by the sun, the sea-air and the march of evolution. The reason Rottnest Island is not known as Quokka Nest Island is because (a) quokka don't make nests and (b) a passing Dutch sea captain[‡] thought they were large rats. The Dutch had been sailing across the Indian Ocean for a fair while but for the most part turned hard a'port before getting to Australia (which wasn't Australia at the time, of course) and heading off northward to plunder the resources of the Dutch East Indies (i.e. Indonesia). Not all of them managed to turn soon enough and plowed bow-first into the coast of (as yet unnamed) Western Australia. This is not quite what happened this time (i.e. 29 December 1696); Vlamingh seems to have just wanted to have a look-see. And did– but he didn't look closely enough at the quokkas. But then he had probably never seen a wallaby, a kangaroo or any sort of marsupial.

Skip ahead a chunk of time and the English eventually turned up with colonisation on their minds. It didn't take them long to work out that Rottnest Island was just the place to incarcerate members of the indigenous people who wilfully insisted on being aboriginal. When the fun in that began to wane, the English overlords turned their attention to the lower-classes and added a reformatory for those children of the lower classes who wilfully insisted on being ill-behaved. Finally, all this sort of ruling-class fun was given up, although residual memories of this use allowed Rottnest to be used as an internment camp in both world wars.

Somewhere along the way, some of the people of Perth, apparently not content with living with their own mainland venomous snakes, lizards, bush flies, heat and sand, decided Rottnest Island was just the place for day trips, weekend visits and school holiday stays. This odd behaviour increased over time despite the primitive accommodation (which included some of the buildings originally part of the prison and reformatory) and singular lack of facilities. And this less-than-prepossessing venue and its less-than-prepossessing regulars, was what Rottnest Island was at the time Lyon and Rattigan decided to use it in the way which will be seen in pages that follow.

To be fair, the view that Lyon and Rattigan (and many others of refined sensibilities) held at the time may well have been transcended in the nearly forty decades since, and it should be noted that the Western Australian Tourist Board (who are, no doubt, quite objective about it) describe Rottnest Island as 'Perth's idyllic island playground'. Which, oddly enough, is an echo of the aforesaid W. Vlamingh, who said (presumably in Dutch) that it was 'a paradise on Earth' – although it is hard to know what he had to compare it with. It is worth noting, he didn't stay. The quokkas did – and still do.

---

* *Thanks, Wikipedia.*
‡ *Willem de Vlamingh, if you must know.*

ROTTNEST ISLAND FILM COMMISSION ARCHIVE

Sadly for researchers, PhD students and archeologists of the future, much of the content of the archives of the Rottnest Island Film Commission has disappeared.

What may exist today in terms of an archive of the Rottnest Island Film Commission consists of a rusty filing cabinet kept in the back shed on the property of Peregrine Gaveston, the longtime companion of Mervyn Whipple, where Whipple lived after his mother died after years of congenital disappointment. Whipple himself died following a botched sex change operation in the Philippines in 2009. (The operation was not on himself.)

It is thought that much Rottnest Island Film Commission material was confiscated in a series of raids over the years of the Commission's existence by officers of either the Australia Intelligence Security Organisation or the Australian Federal Police. If so, the confiscated material was most likely destroyed for security reasons or, conversely, stolen by agents of foreign intelligence agencies. If the latter explanation is true, it is equally as likely the KGB, Mossad, or the CIA destroyed the material themselves out of embarrassment when they, severally, realised how useless it was for any potential covert activities.

Alternative suggestions as to the absence of most of the correspondence between the various governments that came and went in the period of Sir Bruce Fernargle-Jones' tenure as chairman, the total lack of enquiries from the Tax Office, the dearth of account books, financial statements, credit card statements or even cheque butts include (as some have claimed) that most were eaten by Wimpy the piano-playing marsupial when the lettuces ran out, or that Roy Cleghorn denuded the archive of paper in order to supply his sanitary needs on his many sojourns into the bush in search of locations or hiding places.

Whether these or any other conspiracy theories have any validity cannot be firmly established. And neither should they be.

The editor is more that satisfied that most of the material was destroyed on the orders of Sir Bruce Fernargle-Jones' legal advisors for fear of defamation suits from many (if not all) of those mentioned in the first instance on air and now again in the preceding pages. If any reader has been foolish, stalwart or plain pig-headed enough to have read this far, he or she or it will no doubt concur with the editor.

What follows is pretty much what's left.

ROTTNEST ISLAND FILM COMMISSION

EPISODE ONE

by William Lyon and Neil Rattigan

Bert is put out by having his personal territory invaded for business purposes, and the employees of the newly founded Rottnest Island Film Commission gather at their convenience.

CAST OF CHARACTERS

BERT	MERVYN WHIPPLE
ANNOUNCER	TEQUILA MOCKINGBIRD
SIR BRUCE FERNARGLE-JONES	DOLLY MIXTURE

A TOILET OF NO FIXED ABODE.

GRAMS: TWENTIETH CENTURY FOX FANFARE. STARTS FAST AND RUNS DOWN.

F.X.: A MOP BEING SLOPPED IN A BUCKET OF WATER AND BEING SLAPPED AND SWIRLED ON A TILE FLOOR.

BERT: (Singing) Whistle while you work, whistle while you work. (Whistles)

F.X.: FALSE TEETH FLYING OUT OF MOUTH AND LANDING IN TOILET BOWL.

BERT: (incoherent muttering)

F.X.: TEETH BEING PICKED OUT OF TOILET BOWL AND PUT IN MOUTH.

BERT: It's a sorry state of affairs if a man can't have a whistle without his teeth falling in the carsie. A man should write to the Prime Monster.

F.X.:	MOPPING NOISES

BERT: I don't know. Holding a board meeting in a carsie. Lovely state of affairs. In my day, people held their meetings in an orifice. I blames it on Henry Truman and his masonic bomb. A man should write to the Prime Monster.

F.X.: DOOR OPENING. FOOTSTEPS COMING DOWN STAIRS. FOOT STEPPING INTO A BUCKET.

MERVYN: Helloo-oo-oo-oo!

F.X.: BUCKET AND PERSON CRASHING ACROSS FLOOR. CUBICLE DOOR SWINGS VIOLENTLY OPEN. TOILET SEAT CLATTERING. TOILET FLUSHING. PAUSE

MERVYN. Oh. Bucket!

ANNOUNCER: We would just like to interrupt this programme to point out that the word Mr Whipple just used was bucket That is, B-U-C-K-E-T-T. Thank you.

BERT: They ought to look where they are putting their plates of meat. Kicking a man's bucket round like that. Now I'll have to fill it up again.

MERVYN: (incomprehensible mumblings)

F.X.: HIGH-HEELED SHOES WALKING ON TILED FLOOR.

TEQUILA: Are you talking to me? God, I can't understand a word you are saying.

MERVYN: (Mumbles)

TEQUILA: What are you saying? What is he saying? What am I doing here? What did I come in here for?

BERT: To have a poo?

TEQUILA: Are you talking to me?

BERT: No.

F.X.: FALSE TEETH FLYING OUT AND FALLING INTO TOILET BOWL.

TEQUILA: I'm not in a place five minutes before everyone's got their head in the can, man. God, that's tacky.

F.X.: HIGH HEELS ON TILE FLOOR LEAVING.

SIR BRUCE: (Off) I'm sorry. I thought this was the gents'.

TEQUILA: (Off and fading into distance) Are you talking to me? What are you saying? I can't understand a word you are saying.

SIR BRUCE: God heavens, Ripple. What are you doing down there? And I hate that colour of brown tie you are wearing.

MERVYN: But I'm not wearing a tie.

F.X.:   A LAMBRETTA SCOOTER BEING DRAGGED
               DOWN A SET OF STAIRS.

DOLLY: (Breathless). Hello Sir Bruce. Hello Mervyn.
               Hello...er... I would have been here sooner but I got
               my Mikimoto pearls caught in the back wheel of my
               Lambretta.

MERVYN: Could you get your scooter off my foot, do you think?

DOLLY: I don't like that aftershave you're wearing, Mervyn.

MERVYN: I'm not wearing any aftershave.

DOLLY: Then it must be your tie.

F.X.:   AEROSOL SPRAY BEING SPRAYED AROUND
               ROOM.

SIR BRUCE: Good god, Ripple, what are you doing now?

MERVYN: I thought I detected a slight odour.

BERT: A slight odour. My foot.

F.X.:   SLAMMING OF CUBICLE DOOR.

BERT: (Off) My foot died in the war for people like him.

SIR BRUCE: Ripple — and let me make this perfectly clear — I
               should like those lids down, so we can all sit down.

MERVYN: Yes, Sir Bruce. At once, Sir Bruce.

F.X.: TOILET LIDS BEING SLAMMED DOWN ONE AT A TIME.

SIR BRUCE: That's better. Now, Miss Mixture, you sit there.

F.X.: SOUND OF SOMEBODY SITTING ON SHINY VINYL CUSHION

SIR BRUCE: Good god, Miss Mixture. Was that you?

DOLLY: No, Sir Bruce. It was my J-Trel cushion.

GRAMS: COMMERCIAL TYPE INTRODUCTION MUSIC.

ANNOUNCER: Yes. You too can turn your little room into another entertainment centre of your home. With the J-Trel portable carsie cushion. Do you have problems when Grannie comes to stay for Christmas, and your nuclear family has only four chairs? J-Trel has solved your problem. Put Granny, or any other unwanted guest at your convenience and at their ease with J-Trel super-soft, genuine vinyl, multi-coloured, anti-haemorrhoid carsie cushion. Guaranteed to wear out or we'll keep your money. Available at Woolworths, Coles family stores, K Mart, Target and abattoirs everywhere.

TEQUILA: Were they talking to me?

ANNOUNCER: Well! Will Bert forgive the Rottnest Island Film Commission for taking over his toilet?

BERT: No. I won't.

ANNOUNCER: Will Sir Bruce Fernagle-Jones pull the Rottnest Island Film Commission members in line? Were Dolly Mixture's pearls insured? And will Mervyn Whipple get deterred... from the front of his jacket? These questions and many more, will be totally ignored in the next meeting of the Rottnest Island Film Commission, when you will meet Roy Cleghorn, Rex 'Slick' Piranha and other members.

GRAMS: THEME MUSIC. KENNY BALL AND JAZZMEN, 'SOME DAY MY PRINCE WILL COME'. PLAYED AT 45RPM.

END

ROTTNEST ISLAND FILM COMMISSION

EPISODE TWO

by William Lyon and Neil Rattigan

Rex suggests some tax lurks, and tail-less foxes and radio-controlled lemons with duty-free aerials obfuscate the issue. Dolly offers Sir Bruce Fernargle-Jones a ride, but things start to get up his nose.

EPISODE TWO

CAST OF CHARACTERS

BERT	SIR BRUCE FERNARGLE-JONES
REX PIRANHA	TEQUILA MOCKINGBIRD
MERVYN WHIPPLE	DOLLY MIXTURE
ANNOUNCER	

A TOILET OF NO FIXED COMMODE.

GRAMS: TWENTIETH CENTURY FOX FANFARE. STARTS FAST AND RUNS DOWN.

F.X.:   MOP BEING SLOPPED IN A BUCKET OF WATER AND SLAPPED ONTO TILE FLOOR. SWISHING SOUNDS.

BERT: (Sings) Whistle while you work, whistle while you work, (whistles)

F.X.:   FALSE TEETH POPPING OUT OF MOUTH AND FALLING IN TOILET BOWL.

BERT: (Incoherent mumbling)

F.X.:   TEETH BEING PICKED OUT OF BOWL AND PUT INTO MOUTH

BERT: I dragged meself up from the bottom to this job. I was taught in the army that a good mate never leaves his friends behind. And now they are holding board meetings in me carsie — and writing the minutes on the back of the door. At least, I hope it's the minutes that are written there. I'll have to get me National Health glasses.

F.X.:   FOOTSTEPS ENTERING.

SIR BRUCE: (Approaching)...that takes me back to when I was Minister for Aboriginal Affairs.

REX: Yes. I had an aboriginal affair. It was when I had the Classic Vauxhilla Viva, Hillman Imp and Ford Anglia dealership of the Great Southern, Bullaring and Southern Hemisphere area. I moved a lot of stock through my yards. I sold all three cars within six months. And, as you know, Sir Bruce, I have never looked back.

SIR BRUCE: Too bloody right. You wouldn't have dared.

GRAMS: COMMERCIAL TYPE INTRODUCTION MUSIC FADES INTO NATIVE DRUMMING.

VOICE: (Stage African Accent) Hmm. De natives am restless tonight. But dey wouldn't be if dey owning de car from Nkaba Nbebe Vauxhill Viva, Hillman Imp and Ford Anglia dealers ob Nairobi. Ah tellin' my salesmen — we not just sellin' de cars, we car counsellors. We taking on de whole fambly. If dey not happy wid de car, dey findin' demselves hangin' from de rearvision mirror. Dealer licence number...le me tink bout dis...er...number one. Phone number, Nairobi two. Don't ring Nairobi one. It de presidential palace, and my brudder don't take messages for me. De bugger.

TEQUILA: Are you talking to me?

SIR BRUCE: I want to talk to you, Rex, about this company car tax-dodge lurk. I can't keep coming to board meetings on the back of Miss Mixture's Lambretta. The foxtail on the aerial keeps getting up my nose.

BERT: (Off) Well, it's big enough for the rest of the bleeding fox to fit up there as well.

REX: Yes. I could see how that could be a bit of a problem.

SIR BRUCE: What could?

REX: About the fox.

SIR BRUCE: What fox?

REX: Yes.

SIR BRUCE: Oh.

REX: You mean, the car?

SIR BRUCE; What car?

REX: Yes.

SIR BRUCE: Oh.

F.X.:   HIGH HEELED SHOES ENTERING.

DOLLY: Sir Bruce. Have you seen the foxtail off my aerial?

SIR BRUCE: What aerial?

REX: You mean the car.

DOLLY: What car?

REX: Yes.

SIR BRUCE: Oh.

MERVYN: Morning everyone. Look what I just found next to the Flushmatic. A little pussy cat in one of your hankies, Sir Bruce.

SIR BRUCE: What hankie?

MERVYN: This one. With the cat's tail in it.

SIR BRUCE: What cat's tail?

REX: You mean the car.

MERVYN: Oh.

DOLLY: That's off my aerial.

MERVYN: What aerial?'

REX: You mean the car?

SIR BRUCE: No, the scooter.

REX: You want to lease a scooter for tax purposes?

DOLLY: It's a foxtail.

REX: You can't get a foxtail on a tax concession.

DOLLY: But you can get one on an aerial.

MERVYN: You can get a tax concession on an aerial?

REX: No, only on a car.

SIR BRUCE: What car?

MERVYN: The one with the aerial on it.

DOLLY: My scooter has an aerial. Can I get a tax concession on that?

REX: Yes. But only if you have a car attached to it.

SIR BRUCE: What car?

REX: Yes.

SIR BRUCE: Oh.

MERVYN: Why doesn't the Commission get a car, Sir Bruce?

REX: Yes. You could lease it as a tax concession.

SIR BRUCE: Good. That'll save me having to come to meetings on Miss Mixture's Lambretta— and let me make this perfectly clear — stop her foxtail from getting up my nose.

BERT: (off) That's not what gets up my nose, matey.

DOLLY: But I've lost my foxtail, Sir Bruce.

MERVYN: Well, have this one. I just found it.

DOLLY: Ooh. Lovely. It's just like the one I used to have.

REX: Now look here, Sir Bruce. I'm in a position to do you a bit of good.

SIR BRUCE: Good god, Rex. So you are. I didn't know you could do calisthenics.

BERT: (off) If he does it on my nice clean floor, he can clean it up himself.

REX: Just come in here, Sir Bruce, and we'll talk about this.

F.X.: CUBICLE DOOR OPENING AND CLOSING AGAIN

BOTH (mumbling off)

ANNOUNCER: Well! Will Rex Piranna sell the Rottnest Island Film Commission a lemon? Or will they insist upon a car? Can Sir Bruce Fernagle-Jones tell the difference? Or will he have to suck it and see?

SIR BRUCE: Do you have these Commodores in another flavour?

ANNOUNCER: Will the Taxation Department allow full rebate on foxtail aerials on citrus fruit? These questions and many similar will be totally ignored at the next board meeting of the Rottnest Island Film Commission, when in addition to the board members that you know and love, you will meet Roy Cleghorn, Rottnest Island's answer to Harry Butler.

BERT: Here's my answer to Harry Butler. (Raspberry)

DOLLY: Harry Butler doesn't have an aerial.

MERVYN: What aerial?

REX: You mean the car.

SIR BRUCE: Oh.

GRAMS: THEME MUSIC. KENNY BALL AND HIS JAZZMEN, 'SOME DAY MY PRINCE WILL COME' PLAYED AT 45RPM.

END

ROTTNEST ISLAND FILM COMMISSION

EPISODE THREE

by William Lyon and Neil Rattigan

Swan Upping is sent for and Roy Cleghorn puts a cat (marsupial of course) amongst the galahs.

EPISODE THREE

CAST OF CHARACTERS

BERT	QUEEN VICTORIA
SIR BRUCE FERNARGLE-JONES	TEQUILA MOCKINGBIRD
ROY CLEGHORN	MERVYN WHIPPLE
DOLLY MIXTURE	ANNOUNCER
VOICES 1,2,3.	

A TOILET OF NO FIXED INCOME.

GRAMS: TWENTIETH CENTURY FOX FANFARE. STARTS FAST AND RUNS DOWN.

F.X.:   MOP BEING SLOPPED IN A BUCKET OF WATER AND SLAPPED ONTO TILE FLOOR. SWISHING SOUNDS.

BERT: (Sings) Whistle while you work, whistle while you work, (whistles)

F.X.:   FALSE TEETH POPPING OUT OF MOUTH AND FALLING IN TOILET BOWL.

BERT: (Incoherent mumbling)

F.X.:   TEETH BEING PICKED OUT OF BOWL AND PUT INTO MOUTH.

BERT: It's bad enough them having their meetings here, but a man can't turn his bucket for a second ...

F.X:	TYPING UNDER
BERT:	...without they are moving a pornographer in here. What would Queen Victoria – bless her – have said?
GRAMS:	LAND OF HOPE AND GLORY – CONTINUES UNDER
QUEEN:	We are not amused...sailor.
BERT	I ain't no sailor. I died while serving in the King's Own Foot and Mouth Latrine Corps for people like her.
F.X:	LAND OF HOPE AND GLORY UNDER
QUEEN	Not for we, you didn't, matey.
SIR BRUCE:	Oh, Miss Mixture. Take a letter.
DOLLY:	Er...er...Zed. Did I get it right, Sir Bruce? Oh, you're wonderful, Sir Bruce. Such a clever party trick.
SIR BRUCE:	What are you talking about, Miss Mixture? Take these down at once.
DOLLY:	Oh, Sir Bruce. I didn't know you cared.
SIR-BRUCE:	I don't — but I won't have panty-hose hanging off the toilet doors.
DOLLY:	Oh dear. How's a working girl supposed to do her smalls? It's that greasy Lambretta.

BERT:	Serves you right for going out with Italians. I shot at Italians during the war for people like you.
SIR BRUCE:	A memo, Miss Mixture, to Finklestein, Finklestein and Wong, Theatrical agents of Cairo, Egypt. Dear Darryl...
F.X.:	BURST OF TYPING.
SIR BRUCE:	Re your's of fifteenth ultimo, viz-a-viz, ipso factor, therefore, not withstanding, wherein we have hereto for, and without prejudice to a priori arrangements notwithstanding, and in as much as, we have, without malice and aforethought, contracted through and on behalf of the Rottnest Island Film Commission – the party of the first part – and your good selves – the party of the second part – on behalf and without prejudice for, to, or against, Miss Swan Upping – the party of the third part – who, on completion of this agreement, becomes the party of the second. Can Miss Upping start work on Monday? Remind her to bring a cut lunch.
F.X.:	EXTREMELY SHORT TYPING.
DOLLY:	Got that, Sir Bruce.
SIR BRUCE:	Sign that: 'Sir Bruce'.
F.X.:	EXTREMELY LONG TYPING
DOLLY:	Is that all, Sir Bruce? Who was that to, Sir Bruce?

GRAMS:	COMMERCIAL INTRODUCTION MUSIC
VOICE 1:	(Stage Jewish) Oy vay. Finklestein, Finkelstein and Wong, Theatrical Agents — and all kosher ceremonies done cheap. Let us quote you a price that is a cut off the top. Take a tip from us. We slash anything. Discount for anyone who'll mind the shop on Saturdays. Listen to these satisfied customers...
VOICE 2:	(Heavy Scots accent) Och the noo, Jimmy. Ma wee wifey has been gang-awa' pleased with me sporran since I went to Finklestein, Finklestein and Wong. Now I can celebrate two New Years without embarrassment.
VOICE 3:	(Totally indecipherable Chinese sounds except for concluding words)...Finklestein, Finklestein and Wong.
TEQUILA:	Are you talking to me?
GRAMS:	GREIG: 'MORNING' FROM 'PEER GYNT SUITE' UNDER
F.X.:	STOCKWHIPS, KOOKABURRAS AND HOBNAIL BOOTS.
ROY:	Coo-ee, Cobblers.
F.X.:	BODY SLIPPING AND FALLING DOWN STAIRS. THUD. KOOKABURRA BEING SAT ON.

ROY: Ahh. Wombats!

SIR BRUCE: Who is this clod?

MERVYN: (Entering) This clod, Sir Bruce, is Roy Clodhorn...
                er...sorry Cleghorn, noted bushwalker and camper.

SIR BRUCE: Oh, really?

ROY: Oh, cripes, I've landed on me burra.

MERVYN: Roy trained the wombat stampede in 'Picnic at
                Hanging Rock'.

SIR BRUCE: Oh, really?

DOLLY: But there was no wombat stampede in 'Picnic at
                Hanging Rock'.

ROY: No. The bludgers cut it out. That's why we never really
                find out what happened to those sheilas.

SIR BRUCE: Oh, really?

MERVYN: (Whispers) Sir Bruce, Roy is part of the conditions
                under which we were given the grant for that
                ecological film, 'The Wombat That Ate Ayres Rock'.

SIR BRUCE: Let me get this perfectly clear. You mean, in return for
                that massive, non-repayable, government grant, we
                are stuck with this massive nonreturnable idiot?

MERVYN: In a word, and to put it simply, to avoid confusion, and in order to obviate any possible miscomprehension — yes.

SIR BRUCE: Oh.

F.X.: BUCKET BEING KICKED OFF FOOT, ACROSS FLOOR AND SLAMMED INTO WALL.

ROY: G'day, Merve. Cripes, I just come a gutser on me burra. What flaming mongrel left that bucket at the top of the stairs.

BERT: It's alright for you, matey. But this bucket's father died in the war for people like you.

MERVYN: I'd like to meet the Chairman of the Commission. Sir Bruce — Roy.

ROY: G'day Bruce. I think I met your brother in India — Viceroy.

SIR BRUCE: Oh, really?

ROY: Say, Bruce, who's the bonza looking sheila with the legs like a bungarra?

SIR BRUCE: What? Where?

ROY: That sheila over there — with the expression like a startled gardie?

SIR BRUCE: Oh. You mean Miss Mixture, my Girl Friday.

ROY: Cripes. Don't tell me you have a different sheila for each day of the week?

F.X.: HIGH HEELED SHOES APPROACHING.

DOLLY: Sir Bruce...

SIR BRUCE: Miss Mixture, I would like you to meet Roy...er...

ROY: Cleghorn. Cleghorn by name, and Cleghorn by nature (laughs).

DOLLY: Aren't you the Roy Cleghorn that climbed up the Three Sisters?

ROY: Cripes, yeah. As I always say, it's harder getting up the three sisters than down.

SIR BRUCE: Oh, really?

DOLLY: That's nice.

ROY: Look here, Bruce. I've got some really bonza ideas for some fair dinkum films.

ALL: (Gasps of shock, dismay)

F.X.: PEOPLE FAINTING, BODIES COLLAPSING.

ANNOUNCER: Well! Will the Rottnest Island Film Commission really make a film? Or will Roy Cleghorn be bound and gagged, and thrust around the S bend? Will Swan Upping turn up by Monday? And will she bring a cut lunch? These questions, and many similar, will be totally ignored at the next meeting of the Rottnest Island Film Commission – when, in addition to the Board members you know and love (if you happen to be their mothers), you will meet two exciting new members all the way from the Indian sub-continent – by cattle boat.

GRAMS: THEME MUSIC. KENNY BALL AND HIS JAZZMEN, 'SOME DAY MY PRINCE WILL COME' at 45RPM.

END

ROTTNEST ISLAND FILM COMMISSION

EPISODE FOUR

by William Lyon and Neil Rattigan

Sir Bruce Fernargle-Jones has a family reunion. Rex Piranha has a good idea for a film. Dolly Mixture expresses concerned for unclothed cows and the Rottnest Island Film Commission is expanded to take in some Commonwealth brethren.

CAST OF CHARACTERS

BERT	GRANDAD
SIR BRUCE FERNARGLE-JONES	REX PIRANHA
DOLLY MIXTURE	MERVYN WHIPPLE
ROY CLEGHORN	RAMITA
JAMITA	VOICES 1, 2, 3, 4, 5, 6, 7, 8

A TOILET OF NO FIXED PERSUASION

GRAMS: 20TH CENTURY FOX FANFARE. STARTS FAST AND RUNS DOWN.

F.X.:   MOP BEING SLOPPED IN BUCKET, AND THEN SLAPPED DOWN ON A TILE FLOOR. MOP SLAPPED AROUND FLOOR.

BERT: (sings) Whistle while you work, whistle while you work (whistles)

F.X.:   FALSE TEETH POPPING OUT OF MOUTH, FLYING THROUGH AIR AND LANDING IN TOILET BOWL.

BERT: (Incoherent mumbling).

F.X.:   TEETH BEING TAKEN FROM BOWL AND REPLACED IN MOUTH

140

BERT	It's bad enough having Lambretta brake fluid mixed up in your flushmatic, but having to get mashed Kookaburra out of the grouting is when I draw the line. My old Grandad used to say: 'Son, you can always stone the crows, but don't never, don't ever, sit on a kookaburra. They've got ruddy sharp peckers.'
GRANDDAD:	No I didn't. What *I* said was, 'Never get a kooka's pecker up your clacker'.
BERT:	Oh, shut up. (Mumbles into distance) Silly old sod. Who asked him?
F.X:	FOOTSTEPS APPROACHING
SIR BRUCE:	Look, Rex. Putting a sawn-off rocking horse head in my bed last night is not going to work. And telling me that you have 'got' my mother, when I know perfectly well — and she knows perfectly well — that she's been dead for thirty years, is not going to work either. I am not — and let me make myself perfectly clear — I am not going to buy that second hand Rolls Royce.
REX:	But, Sir Bruce. You have got me all wrong. It's not how you think. I am not trying to get you to *buy* a car from me. I am trying to get you to lease a car from me.
SIR BRUCE:	Look here, Rex. If I do get the Commission to lease this car from you, will you put my mother back where you found her?
F.X.:	HOBNAIL BOOTS APPROACHING

ROY: Hey, Rex. I just saw your wife waiting in your car outside.

REX: My wife? She's not in the car. It's her day for selling encyclopaedias today.

GRAMS: COMMERCIAL INTRODUCTION MUSIC.

ANNOUNCER: When were you last embarrassed by being unable to answer questions like these:

VOICE 1: What's a Grecian urn?

VOICE 2: Columbus discovered America by mistake — how big a mistake was this?

VOICE 3: What's a Spanish Armada, and how many of them to the kilo?

ANNOUNCER: Do you have facts like this at your fingertips?

VOICE 4: Noah's Ark was made of wood; and Joan of Ark was Maid of Orleans.

ANNOUNCER: These and many more totally irrelevant and inaccurate pieces of hearsay, contention, and pure, unadulterated lies can be yours by purchasing, in six million weekly instalments, the new Arthur Murray's Idiots Encyclopaedia. Send us a banker's order for your entire income for the rest of your life. Or tear out the coupon from Idiots Weekly (incorporating Moronic Monthly). Hear what these people have said about the new Arthur Murray's Idiots Encyclopaedia: John Kerr — former public servant;

VOICE 5:   (Drunken slur) Helped me make important political decisions.

ANNOUNCER: Ronnie Raygun — political impersonator.

VOICE 6:   (American) I always look up the proper name of world leaders in my Arthur Murray's Encyclopaedia.

ANNOUNCER: James Carter — redundant president.

VOICE 7:   (Southern American drawl) I-all would never have'n called him John, if'n I'd had an Arthur Murray's Encyclopaedia, y'all.

ANNOUNCER: Idi Amin — former heavyweight boxer and humanitarian:

VOICE 8:   (African) Everything I did, I did because of Arthur Murray.

ANNOUNCER: Don't delay. Send today for your beautifully bound — with a genuine copper staple — first issue of Arthur Murray's Idiots Encyclopaedia.

ROY: Well, if it isn't the little woman, it's certainly a bonza looking sheila.

REX: Oh...er...that's...er...that's Raylene Stokegobbler. I was...er...thinking of trying her out... for a part in the documentary on nude wrestling actually, Sir Bruce.

SIR BRUCE: Oh, really. I'll go and check out her parts myself.

F.X.:	FOOTSTEPS LEAVING
DOLLY	That's nice.
ROY:	I didn't know that we were making a doco on nude wrestling, Rex.
REX:	Oh. I just thought of it last night actually.
DOLLY;	I don't think that nude rustling is such a good idea for a film, Mr Piranha.
REX:	Why not?
DOLLY:	I think the cows should have at least a little bell to wear, for modesty's sake. And wouldn't the pommel on the saddle endanger the cowboy's future prospects if they came off?
ROY:	Starve the lizards. What is she going on about?
F.X.:	FOOTSTEPS ENTERING
MERVYN:	Has anyone seen Sir Bruce?
BERT:	He's a tall bloke with grey hair and shoulder-length eyebrows.
DOLLY:	Do you think that horses get embarrassed standing naked in front of cows?

REX:	Only when the Isle of Wight ferry arrives?
ROY:	Sir Bruce is outside...getting the lay of the land.
DOLLY:	Do you think that cowboys get embarrassed standing naked in front of cows?
REX:	Only when the Royal Yacht arrives.
MERVYN:	Well, Mr. Ramita and Mr. Jamita have just arrived in the taxi outside. I think Sir Bruce should be here to meet them.
F.X.:	SOUNDS OF FISTICUFFS, HITTING. BODIES FALLING DOWN STAIRS.
BERT:	Watch out for me bucket.
F.X.:	BUCKET BEING KICKED. SCUFFLING.
BERT:	Look what you've done. In your country a family of twenty-four could've lived in that bucket - and you've dented it.
RAMITA:	Look what you are doing to my turban. It's all coming unravelled and sticking up my dhoti.
JAMITA:	I've fallen down those stairs because of your rotting turban. Allah be praised — I could have been given a cerebral haemorrhoid.

RAMITA:	I am wishing you had. Your last film is looking as if you did have a cerebral haemorrhoid — and they removed your brain to stop it spreading.
JAMITA:	May all your children be born with three heads — and you are going bankrupt buying them turbans.
F.X. :	HITTING AND SCUFFLING UNDER
BOTH:	(Incoherent cries and groans)
DOLLY:	Oh, Mervyn. Who are these exotic gentlemen in bed sheets hitting each other?
MERVYN:	Gentlemen. Please. I'd like you to meet Miss Dolly Mixture.
F.X.:	FIGHTING AND SCUFFLING CEASES
RAMITA:	Oh, my goodness. A woman. Be getting out of my way. I must be slobbering over her.
MERVYN:	These are the two gentlemen who will be joining the Commission. India's leading clapper/loader, Mr. Ramita. And India's leading focus/puller, Mr. Jamita.
DOLLY:	Oh. I went to India once. I won a trip on the Adelaide Steamship Company.
ROY:	Yeah. I bet you couldn't get an Indian boomerang.
DOLLY:	No. But I did get dysentery.

REX: Yes, I've heard it runs in your family.

ANNOUNCER: Well! Will Sir Bruce's mother get re-interred? Or will he lease that new car and keep her in the ashtray? Will Dolly be able to tell Ramita from Jamita? Would your mother allow *you* to see a film that contained full-frontal bovine nudity? Can horses really wrestle naked? These questions and others nothing like them will be completely ignored at the next meeting of the Rottnest Island Film Commission.

GRAMS: THEME MUSIC: KENNY BALL AND HIS JAZZMEN, 'SOME DAY MY PRINCE WILL COME', PLAYED AT 45RPM.

END

ROTTNEST ISLAND FILM COMMISSION

EPISODE FIVE

by William Lyon and Neil Rattigan

In which consternation is caused by the arrival of a letter from the
Council for the Arts, Marlene Dietrich is confused with Carmen
Miranda, physics professors are sent packing and strange things are
done with folded paper.

EPISODE FIVE

CAST OF CHARACTERS

BERT
MARLENE DIETRICH   SIR BRUCE FERNARGLE-JONES
REX PIRANHA   DOLLY MIXTURE
MERVYN WHIPPLE   ROY CLEGHORN
RAMITA   JAMITA
TEQUILA MOCKINGBIRD   ANNOUNCER
MUM   DAD
PHYSICS PROFESSOR

A TOILET OF NO FIXED SENSIBILITY

GRAMS: 20TH CENTURY FOX FANFARE. STARTS FAST
               AND RUNS DOWN.

F.X.:   MOP BEING SLOPPED IN BUCKET, AND THEN
               SLAPPED DOWN ON A TILE FLOOR. MOP
               SLAPPED AROUND FLOOR.

BERT: (sings) Whistle while you work, whistle while you
               work (whistles)

F.X.:   FALSE TEETH POPPING OUT OF MOUTH, FLYING
               THROUGH AIR AND LANDING IN TOILET BOWL.

BERT: (Incoherent mumbling).

F.X.:   TEETH BEING TAKEN FROM BOWL AND
               REPLACED IN MOUTH.

BERT: I'm fed up with having to get me national health choppers out of the loo every week just for a cheap joke. I'm going to sing something else from now on. (Sings) 'Falling in love again, never wanted to, what am I to do, I can't help it.' I wonder what ever happened to that lovely Marlene Dirtrack. Never mind about this Swan Upping bint. They ought to get Marlene for their pictures. Yers, I remember her. I wonder if she remembers me?

GRAMS: ROMANTIC MUSIC.

MARLENE: Bert. How could I ever forget you? How well I remember those nights in the Casbah.

BERT: Oh, yers. In Ali Fiessel's combined Cabaret, Gambling Casino and Chinese Laundry. Ali cleaned out the towels, you cleaned out the tables, and I cleaned out the t...t...troublemakers.

MARLENE: Oh, mon petite, how my heart throbs at the sight of your little...toilet brush. You get into the S bend of my heart.

GRAMS: MARLENE DIETRICH SINGING 'FALLING IN LOVE AGAIN' WITH OVER...

BERT: (Sings) Falling in Love again. Never wanted to, what am I to do? I can't help it.

GRAMS: MARLENE DIETRICH GRADUALLY FADES OUT

BERT:	(Still singing) Men gather to me, like moths around the flame, and if their wings burn, I know I'm not to blame. (Fades into the distance.)
F.X. :	FOOTSTEPS – MALE and FEMALE
DOLLY:	That's funny, Sir Bruce. I could have sworn that I heard Marlene Dietrich's voice a moment ago.
SIR BRUCE:	Oh, really? *I* thought it sounded more like Carmen Miranda.
DOLLY	Oh, no, Sir Bruce. Carmen Miranda sounds like this.
GRAMS:	CARMEN MIRANDA SINGING 'Yi Yi Yi Yi Like You Very Much'.
SIR BRUCE:	That's very good, Miss Mixture. How did you do that?
DOLLY:	Do what, Sir Bruce?
SIR BRUCE	Sound like Marlene Dietrich.
F.X.:	FOOTSTEPS ENTERING UNDER
DOLLY:	You mean, sound like Carmen Miranda.
REX:	Marlene Dietrich doesn't sound like Carmen Miranda. Carmen Miranda sounds like this.
GRAMS:	FIRST MOVEMENT OF CARL ORFF's 'Carmina Birana'.

SIR BRUCE: Now, that sounds like Marlene Dietrich.

ANNOUNCER: Sir Bruce unfortunately is mistaken. That was in fact not Carmen Miranda, but Carmina Birana, a cantata written by Carl Orff. Just to help you distinguish: Carmina Birana sounds like this...

GRAMS: 'CARMINA BIRANA'.

ANNOUNCER: And Carmen Miranda sounds like this...

GRAMS: BERT FROM *SESAME STREET* SINGING 'RUBBER DUCKY'.

ANNOUNCER: And Marlene Dietrich sounds like this...

GRAMS: MARLENE DIETRICH SINGING 'FALLING IN LOVE AGAIN'.

ANNOUNCER: And my mother-in-law sounds like this ...

F.X.:   RASPBERRY

ANNOUNCER: I hope that is all perfectly clear.

BERT: How's a bloke supposed to get any work done with all these bleeding pineapples and coffee beans all over the place? I died in the war for lack of a decent cup of coffee and a 'nana.

SIR BRUCE:	Look here, enough of this terpischorean prattle. There are matters of — and let me make this perfectly clear — matters of great importance to discuss. I think that it's about time we instigated a Board meeting...

ALL TOGETHER

ROY:	Stone the Crows
REX:	Are you mad?
DOLLY:	That's nice, dear.
MERVYN:	I feel faint....

F.X.:	BODY FALLING ON HARD FLOOR. TOILETS FLUSHING UNCONTROLLABLY.

DOLLY:	Sir Bruce, Mr. Whipple's fainted. Have you any smelling salts?

BERT:	I've got a smelly dunny brush. I'll put that under his bugle.

MERVYN:	(Gasping and spluttering noises. Low moans).

SIR BRUCE:	Just put him on the chaise longue.

ROY:	Fair suck of the sauce bottle, Bruce. What's this meeting caper all about then?

RAMITA:	The last time I am hearing about a meeting, it is about the partitioning of India. Things are not going rightly ever sincing.

JAMITA:	If this meeting is to discuss your partitioning. I am voting in favour, and supplying my own little scimitar personally.

F.X.:	SOUNDS OF HITTING AND SCUFFLING.
BOTH:	Cries of: 'take that', and vague insults and groans.
SIR BRUCE:	Gentlemen. This is not the time, nor indeed, the place for a display of pugilistic aggression. Mr Ramita, would you please remove your foot from Mr Jamita's windpipe. And Mr Jamita, would you please try to stop stuffing Mr Ramita's turban down his throat.
DOLLY:	Oh, don't these little Indian people have a glorious culture to draw upon. They can do such wonderful things with their hands, can't they? (Shrieks).
SIR BRUCE:	Now, let's get this meeting to order, please.
REX:	I'll have fish and chips.
SIR BRUCE:	Rex, we all know that your last project was as a gagwriter for the Don Lane Show. But this is no time for a display of antiquarian humour. This, gentlemen – and let me make this perfectly clear – is serious.
MERVYN:	(Waking up) Oh dear. I felt a little queer.
DOLLY:	Yes, I went out last night too. I had a lovely time. I went to the Margaret Fulton Remedial School for Cooking and Applied Physics.
GRAMS:	COMMERCIAL TYPE INTRODUCTION MUSIC.
F.X.	DOOR CHIMES, FOOTSTEPS, DOOR OPENING.

CHILD: Ooh, Mum.

MUM: (Terry Jones voice) What Now? (From distance)

CHILD;   There's a grotty old physics professor at the door.

MUM: (distant) Not another one. What's he want?

CHILD: He says he wants a boiled egg and a milk bottle.

MUM: (approaching) Do you think we are made of milk bottles? You're the third one this week. I've got a kitchen full of milk bottles with eggs stuffed in them.

PROFESSOR: But Madam, there is a glass and a half...

MUM: Oh yes, you physics professors are all very clever at putting boiled eggs into bottles, but not so clever at getting them out again.

PROFESSOR: There is a whole glass and a half of milk in every block of...

MUM: Oh, yes. I'm not surprised with all the milk bottles chock full of hard-boiled eggs;

DAD: Yes, Professor, but it's the flavour that gets me.

PROFESSOR: Of course, but it's also the nutrition...

MUM: Don't encourage him. He'll be in my kitchen like a
                  Cruise missile, attracting black pepper onto my
                  spoons, and crushing tin-cans in me sink, and
                  frightening the kids with tales of nuclear fission.

ANNOUNCER: Yes, keep unwanted, octagenarian physics professors
                  out of your kitchen. Keep plenty of Clogberry's milk
                  chocolate on hand. Feed it to your children every day.
                  Watch their pimples develop and their teeth decay.

PROFESSOR: (Sleazy) Hey kid. You want to see me demonstrate
                  atmospheric pressure? You like chocolate, huh?

MUM: No you don't! Get off out of it. Go on, clear off!

F.X.:   DOOR SLAMS.

MUM: What has your father told you about talking to strange
                  scientists?

F.X.:   CHILD BEING HIT ON THE EAR.

SIR BRUCE: If we can get on. I am in receipt of a communication
                  from the Council for the Arts.

ROY: Starve the lizards. Who are they?

MERVYN: They are the government body who have been
                  providing us with large grants, and huge subsidies for
                  making films.

ROY: Cripes. That can't be right. We haven't made any
                  films.

SIR BRUCE:	Precisely. That, Roy, is a remarkably astute and accurate summation, summary-wise, of the current dilemma, problem-wise, with which we, namely the Rottnest Island Film Commission — and let me make this perfectly clear — of which every person here today is a member. That is, excepting, of course, Miss Mixture and Mr. Whipple who are employees of the Rottnest Island Film Commission, of which the rest of us, then, are members. Am I being perfectly clear?
RAMITA:	All this is as clear to me as the Ganges River is after the monsoon is washing away all the top soil — and whole villages as well.
JAMITA:	The monsoon is also sweeping away all the people from the villages too. My brother-in-law — the estate agent — will be only too pleased to be selling you a bungalow on the banks of the Ganges in time for the next monsoon season.
TEQUILA:	Are you talking to me?
JAMITA:	No, I am talking to him.
RAMITA:	I can't understand a word you are saying.
JAMITA:	Perhaps you are understanding this.
F.X.:	SOUNDS OF HITTING, SCUFFLING, FLUSHING TOILETS.
BOTH:	Cries of 'taking this', moans and shouts. (Fade into background)

REX: Now, look here, Sir Bruce.

SIR BRUCE: Good god, Rex. That's not a fit sight for a mason to gaze upon.

DOLLY: Oh, I didn't know you could do origami with that.

MERVYN: Oh yes. You can do paper folding with any sort of paper. Even toilet paper.

ROY: Yes. But it gives you a very limp cocky.

DOLLY: Now, I usually like to make a flying swan.

BERT: Duck!

F.X.: SOUND OF SOMETHING LARGE AND SOGGY HITTING A WALL.

ANNOUNCER: Well! Will Sir Bruce get the letter from the Council for the Arts read? Or will it be folded into a cute little doggie? Will the Rottnest Island Film Commission succeed in passing a motion? How do you get hard-boiled eggs out of milk bottles? Will Ramita and Jamita stop pounding the crud out of each other long enough to pull...focus on a Rottnest Island sound stage? Or will the stage leave without them? These questions and a few unrelated to them by blood or law will be treated with contempt in the next meeting of the Rottnest Island Film Commission.

REX: (off) I haven't got a very big part this week.

BERT:	(Faint) You ain't got a very big part any time.

GRAMS:	THEME MUSIC. KENNY BALL AND JAZZMEN, 'SOMEDAY MY PRINCE WILL COME' PLAYED AT 45 RPM.

END

Editor – Perhaps a word of explanation is needed. The 'Professor' character is this script was intended to be a send up of a certain Professor Julius Summer Miller who, as Wikipedia reminds us, 'was an American physicist and television personality. He is best known for his work on children's television programs in North America and Australia'. At the height of his fame, he became a shill for Cadbury chocolate in TV commercials built partly around his scientific 'tricks', including getting a hard-boiled egg into a milk bottle. (Yes, milk came in bottles in those long-ago days.) In 2013 a similar character with a similar (fictional) television history, 'Professor Proton', was played by Bob Newhart in episodes of THE BIG BANG THEORY. These portrayals won Newhart an Emmy Award, but Lyon and Rattigan had the idea first – although it seems the real-life television scientist The Big Bang Theory references is not the same one Rattigan and Lyon allude to.

In addition to sending prospective producers the scripts reproduced above, the writers routinely sent more information. This included lists of the characters that would or potentially might appear in the various episodes. Not all of the characters on the lists appear – only five scripts for radio were written. The descriptions were mainly intended for further comic affect since, if produced, they would 'exist' of disembodied radio actors' voices and physical descriptions were redundant. According to the records in the archive, the list below accompanied submissions made in 1981.

MAIN CHARACTERS

The main characters of The Rottnest Island Film Commission are all members of the Board of Directors. There are also several permanent employees of the Commission. The Rottnest Island Film Commission has also made a practise of endeavouring to attract, on short-term contracts, well-known cinema practitioners from overseas.

CHAIRMAN OF THE BOARD OF DIRECTORS: SIR BRUCE FERNARGLE-JONES

Born in Hay St. Subiaco, but a policeman asked his mother to move on. She did, leaving him with the Policeman.

He was brought up by the Little Sisters of Flagellation and graduated from Kindergarten aged 15, with a major in Finger-painting.

He immediately enlisted to serve in the Boer War, but on being informed that it had been over for forty years, he entered Cox Knob Agricultural College where he pioneered practical research into oral methods of pig castration.

He fought with Montgomery in the desert, with Mountbatten in Burma, McArthur in the Philippines, and with a bald-headed midget called Ernie Blurtt behind the Railway Hotel, Barrack St. Perth.

He was mentioned, disparagingly, in Despatches three times.

He was awarded a D.S.O. by clerical error in 1946.

On learning, in 1953, that World War 2 was over, he left the services.

Having had nothing to do with the cinema in his long and remarkably undistinguished career, Sir Bruce was the obvious candidate for the inaugural chairmanship of the Rottnest Island Film Commission.

In 1976, by another remarkably coincidental clerical error, he was knighted.

MEMBERS OF THE BOARD OF DIRECTORS
REX 'SLICK' PIRANNA

Rex Piranna has not slept very well for twenty years — on the advice of his accountants.

He is a former Pre-owned car salesman ('I wouldn't sell you a car I would sell myself').

Now the International Promotions Head in charge of promoting the Commission's Internationally-acclaimed, award-winning products — and that's no mean feat (there are none).

He was employed because of his unique talents to brown-nose his way into colour supplements, film festivals, and to argue convincingly for non-specific, non-repayable government grants.

He knows nothing about films and has never sat through a film completely – sober or otherwise – but he is aware of every tax dodge and loophole known to man or beast.

ROY CLEGHORN

Roy Cleghorn is a noted bush-walker and camper.

He claims to have taught Harry Butler and the Leyland Brothers everything they know (and a few things that they don't) about negotiating lucrative media deals. He trained the wombat stampede for the classic Australian silent film, *Last In the Bush* (1922), but sadly this climatic scene was edited from the released version due to ecclesiastical protests. The film has now been lost, and archivists and researchers in cinema history all over Australia are extremely grateful.

As a noted animal trainer, Roy Cleghorn was responsible for --------'s* sterling performance in *Storm Boy*. As Roy says, 'It was no mean feat to stop him coming down to the motel pool and drinking it. Let alone breaking the little bugger of the habit of spearing the leather suitcases.'

A native of the land of the Rising Pineapple, Roy believes in defending his women folk with guns and attacking them with clubs.
name deleted for politically correct reasons – editor.

WAYNE BERTOLUCCI

Wayne Bertolucci is an Italian Film Director and fruit shop owner of South Fremantle ('Some of my favourite bits of the world are in South Fremantle'). Due to an unfortunate accident occurring to one of the senior members of his family – that is, accidentally standing in a tub of concrete which happened, equally accidentally, to be dropped into the harbour – Wayne has found he has become a proud Godparent. This doesn't leave him much time for his neo-realistic film pursuits.

ARTHUR DIRECTOR

Arthur Director is the musical co-ordinator of the Rottnest Island Film Commission. He is also a composer and founder of the Elvira Goatbasket Trio.

He started his musical career at an early age, when at the age of six years and seven months, he was trodden upon by the entire Perth Salvation Army Citadel Marching Band.

Over a long and relatively obscure career, his major influences have been the work and plagiarism of John Williams.

Since installation of his silicone-chip, solar-powered hearing aid, his composing ability has leapt forward, and he can now be ranked among Australia's foremost composers – by himself.

He has played Kazoo with the following bands:

Marcia Hines-Goatbasket Trio;
Mark Holden-Goat Basket Trio;
Dawn Frazer-Goatbasket Trio;
Joan Sutherland-Goatbasket Trio;
Rolf Harris-Goatbasket Trio; [*now redacted from his resume*]
Burke and Wills-Goatbasket Trio.

EMPLOYEES OF ROTTNEST ISLAND FILM COMMISSION
MERVYN WHIPPLE: PERSONAL ASSISTANT TO THE CHAIRMAN
Mervyn Whipple is a person of genteel habits and refinement. He suffered a traumatic childhood – that is, he was continually beaten up by the other boys at school and usually on the very same day, he was also beaten up by the girls. Though, as he has since stated, he got quite used to it and began to find it quite enjoyable. His mother had a significant influence over him but since joining the Commission he has been able to exercise a degree of independence; so much so, that he is now allowed to sleep in his own room and in his own bed. Originally appointed as costume designer and wardrobe mistress to the Commission he has expanded his duties to include that of personal assistant to the Chairperson Sir Bruce Fernargle-Jones, or as Mervyn himself puts it – 'Wherever Sir Bruce needs a hand I'm always more than willing to put mine there!'

DOLLY MIXTURE: SECRETARY TO THE CHAIRMAN
Dolly Mixture was voted the original 'Miss Twin-set of 1933'.

As a secretary and mother, she was the victim of a particularly unfortunate administrative error recently and has only just completed her national service for the second time.

BERT

Bert (nobody knows his last name if indeed he has one) is not really an employee of the Rottnest Island Film Commission. When the Commission moved into its new premises, a below-ground men's convenience in the central city, Bert was found already in attendance as a cleaner, carrying on a noble family tradition.

Bert refuses to leave and therefore is ignored by everybody including himself. As near as can be ascertained from his constant mumbling, Bert has served King and Country in every war since the Crimea, and is fully confident of serving in the next one.

VISITING OVERSEAS EXPERTS
RAMITA

Ramita has left the Luton and Districts Bus Line and has come to Australia to join the Rottnest Island Film Commission on an exchange scheme. An Anglo-Indian director of some repute, Ramita directed the musical adaptation of the life of Enoch Powell. A recognised auteur, he is credited with one hundred and fifty films produced in India between the 2nd and the 4th of February 1978 which includes his crowning cinematic achievement the Hindu version of *Saturday Night Fever* starring Kamahl.

JAMITA

Jamita is another Wog.

NOSMO KING

Nosmo King is Britain's leading pornographer but unfortunately is in prison.

REJECTION 1.0

Australian
Broadcasting
Commission

145-149
Elizabeth St.
Sydney
G.P.O. Box 487
2001

Ref. SB:JG

23rd July, 1982

Mr. Neil Rattigan,
24 Wattle Street,
SOUTH PERTH. 6151

Dear Mr. Rattigan,

We have kept the typescripts of your Rottnest Island
Film Commission scripts for a very long time and
I apologise for that, particularly as I must now
tell you that we do not think them suitable for
broadcast in any of our present programs.

It is felt that although the scripts are presented
in radio terms most of the gags are rendered so
visually that the series would sit more happily
on a television screen.

As there were some changes in the programming of
comedy we held the scripts for further consideration,
but I'm afraid that now all we can do is return
them to you.

Thank you for letting us read your sketches; the
typescript is enclosed.

Yours sincerely,

Shan Benson
Radio Drama & Features

Grace Gibson Radio Productions

27th January, 1982

Mr Neil Rattigan
Meded
24 Wattle Street
SOUTH PERTH   WA   6151

Dear Neil,

As promised, we have gone through your scripts of the
"ROTTNEST ISLAND FILM COMMISSION" and while there is
a lot we can enjoy personally, the dialogue and
situations would never be acceptable to commercial radio.

There are a number of good points:-

    1]   The idea.
    2]   You are writing about something you
               know about.
    3]   Writing ability.

On the minus:-

    1]   Scripts should run only 2-3 minutes.
    2]   How would Western Australia accept the
               programme.
    3]   Language.
    4]   Some Offensive situations.
    5]   Writing about audience.
    6]   Too visual.

This criticism is meant to be constructive and hope you
will try another idea or get this one out of the toilet.

Kind regards
GRACE GIBSON RADIO PRODUCTIONS

Reg James
Reg James
Manager

RJ:np

A division of Capital City Broadcasters Pty. Limited
77 Pacific Highway, North Sydney, 2060. Australia
Telephone (02) 922 5533 Telex 24222

Given the failure to convince radio producers of the urgency to part with a few dollars to encourage Lyon and Rattigan to embellish Australian airwaves with an endless stream of episodes of Rottnest Island Film Commission *(the writers had envisioned in their febrile imaginations a radio existence equal to or exceeding that of* Blue Hills*), *they decided to follow the hint given by Shan Benson of ABC Radio Drama and Features that 'the series would sit more happily on a television screen'. (See above.)*

Overlooking the possibility (even probability) that Mr Benson was simply endeavouring through his remarks to soften the blow of telling them to buzz off and not bother him again, Lyon and Rattigan determined to manipulate, massaged mutate the Rottnest Island Film Commission concept and existing (albeit rejected) radio scripts into a television series.

There exist in the archives a surprising (depressing?) number of draft television scripts, most knee-deep so to speak in pencilled and inked amendments, alterations, deletions and obscure editorial hieroglyphics. The script that follows is the only one existing that is complete and unadulterated. It is not clear, however, if this is actually a copy of a script submitted to the ABC and, surprisingly given the cultural context of the material, to a least one British television channel (see Rejection 2.0 below). If this is the submitted script, it would seem that Lyon and Rattigan had rather grandiose ideas of the series as the script is too long for a 'mere' 30-minute television programme. And too elaborate in production terms for the same sort of programming. As will be seen in Rejection 2 below, the Mr John O'Grady of the ABC thought so too. There is some vague circumstantial evidence that this particular version of the script may in fact have been modified into two episodes of shorter duration but, if so, no shorter versions survive in the archive.

The script below is reproduced to give some sense of what Lyon and Rattigan were 'playing at' in writing the Rottnest Island Film

Commission for television. It also represents the Rottnest Island Film Commission's 'last hurrah' – other than for frequent references at much later dates in Sir Bruce Fernargle-Jones' radio talks.

* For those unfortunate souls unfamiliar with Blue Hills, it is recommended that they seek out the Wikipedia entry on it. Suffice it to say here that it ran on ABC radio for 27 years and clocked up 5,795 episodes – at least according to Wikipedia it did, so that must be correct.

ROTTNEST ISLAND FILM COMMISSION

A SERIES FOR TELEVISION

EPISODE TWO

© 1983

1   A TELEVISION STATION IDENTITY CARD: 'NEWS FLASH'

ANNOUNCER
(voice over)
We interrupt this program for a special news report.

2   INT.   TELEVISION NEWS SET

ARLENE FARQUHAR (intense if bland news reader) sits in front of a background containing a subtle station logo pattern.

ARLENE
In Canberra tonight, while the whole country waits expectantly, the debate over the controversial appointment of Sir Bruce Fernargle-Jones continues in the House. The Minister for Cultural Affairs and Public Hygiene, James Stotegobbler, defended the appointment of Sir Bruce as Chairperson of the newly created Rottnest Island Film Commission.

BLUE SCREEN GRAPHICS: STILLS OF PARLIAMENT HOUSE, JAMES STOTEGOBBLER AND SIR BRUCE.

ARLENE
(cont'd)
Mr Stotegobbler told the House that he could not understand how the opposition could seize upon the simple fact that Sir Bruce was a proven liar, cheat, fraud and ne'er-do-well who had never done an honest day's work in his life, and then state that this was some flimsy reason why Sir Bruce should not occupy a responsible government position involving millions of tax dollars. We cross live to Parliament House.

3   EXT.   FRONT OF PARLIAMENT HOUSE

JAMES STOTEGOBBLER stands just outside the revolving doors. He responds to an unseen reporter. A number of microphones and tape recorders are being thrust into his face.

> STOTEGOBBLER
> ...the thinking people of this country can immediately see the benefits that a man of Sir Bruce Fernargle-Jones's calibre brings to such an enterprise. When Sir Bruce talks, people listen.

4   EXT.   A MAIN HIGHWAY

ANGLE: SIR BRUCE's terrified screaming face.
ANGLE: DOLLY and Sir Bruce, on Dolly's Lambretta weave at speed through peak hour traffic. Sir Bruce clings on for dear life.

5   INT.   FILM COMMISSION MAIN OFFICE

BERT stands on a large, executive style chair, placed directly in front of the door. He attempts to mop the ceiling, a task made no easier by the way in which the chair swivels.

MERVYN walks in the front door, stares at Bert, and tugs at his baggy trousers in the area of his bum. Bert reacts by leaping on Mervyn, trying to thrust his mop down Mervyn's throat. Mervyn is dropped to the floor.

> BERT
> Take that, you dirty, filthy great Arab!

He realises who it is and stops.

> BERT
>
> Never sneak up on a man who has spent most of his life defending the back passages of Queen and Country.

Mervyn struggles to his feet, while Bert leans on his mop in story-teller mode.

> BERT
>
> Just me trusty weapon in my hands and a crate of vaseline between me and the whirling dervish hordes, eager for a go at unsullied white flesh. No quarter given, well, not without a struggle, and...

Mervyn points at the chair and at a new desk.

> MERVYN
>
> What's this?

> BERT
>
> Sometimes it took two of us, which was better than doing it by myself. (PAUSE) That. That's a chair. And this here's a desk.

Mervyn sits in the chair and sensually runs his hands over the desk top.

> MERVYN
>
> Oh, tactility plus. There's nothing quite like the feel of new government issue furniture.

BERT

Them dervishes might have had other thoughts about that. And you don't have to mop it, do you, mate?

Bert climbs onto the chair, narrowly avoiding treading on Mervyn's groin and onto the table. He mops the top.

MERVYN

Government supplies turning up when ordered. Down to me. I can see I am going to have a big impact around here.

DOLLY and SIR BRUCE burst into the office on Dolly's Lambretta, which collides with the chair. Mervyn hurtles over the desk, through Bert's legs and into a cupboard on the other side of the office. Sir Bruce falls off the back of the Lambretta on his backside.

SIR BRUCE

Another excellent one-point landing, Miss Mixture.

DOLLY

I do seem to be able to hit the bull's eye, don't I?

Sir Bruce rubs his bum ruefully.

SIR BRUCE

Brown eye, I think, is more apposite.

DOLLY

Mr Yamamoto always said I was potentially his best candidate.

SIR BRUCE

I don't quite comprehend the nippish allusion you
are making.

DOLLY

Yes, you do. Remember the non-specific grant we
received so I could learn to drive after the donkey
died?

SIR BRUCE

Ah, the good days on the Dingo Express Postal
Research Commission.

DOLLY

I spent the whole fifteen thousand dollars on
lessons at the Yamamoto Imperial School of
Driving.

6   INT.   TELEVISION NEWS SET

ARLENE sits at the news desk.

BLUE SCREEN GRAPHIC: JAPANESE FLAG WITH WORLD
WAR TWO AEROPLANE

ARLENE

Memories of World War Two were revived today
when the Federal Police arrested the owner of the
Yamamoto Imperial Japanese School of Driving.

7   EXT. SMALL ODDLY ORIENTAL-LOOKING BUILDING

The building has a large sign: 'Yamamoto Imperial Japanese
School of Driving'.

HAND HELD FOOTAGE:
SEVERAL BURLY POLICEMEN drag an ELDERLY JAPANESE
GENERAL (in full dress uniform) out of the building and into
the back of a police car.

> ARLENE
> (voice over)
> Field Marshal Tojo Yamamoto was allegedly sent on
> a secret mission to Australia over fifty years ago.
> That mission: to create a fifth column, teach
> kamikaze driving methods to cause chaos on the
> roads and disrupt military and civilian road
> communications during the war.

8   INT.   TELEVISION NEWS SET

ARLENE at her desk, reading from an off-screen teleprompter.

BLUE SCREEN GRAPHIC: Car crashing into a caravan a la *Mad Max*

> ARLENE
> Mr Yamamoto established his clandestine
> operation opposite an RSL Club and therefore
> remained unaware that the war had ever ended.
> Police only became aware of the operation when Mr
> Yamamoto commenced advertising on television.

9   EXT. SMALL ODDLY ORIENTAL-LOOKING BUILDING DAY

ANGLE: JAPANESE CAR.
ANGLE WIDENS TO REVEAL: YAMAMOTO IN UNIFORM.

YAMAMOTO

Banzai, folks. I'm General Tojo Yamamoto of Imperial Japanese School of Driving. For only your total unthinking obedience to sacred emperor and several household gods, I can teach to be offensive driver. Surprise friends and loved ones, or people next door. Drive into their home in one of these.

He points at the car.

YAMAMOTO
(cont'd)

Of course, they be even more astonished if you don't tell them you coming. See me today and I soon have you driving like divine wind. Sayonara.

He bows impressively.

10 EXT. SMALL ODDLY ORIENTAL-LOOKING BUILDING DAY

ARREST SCENE
FAT COP stands in front of police car with YAMAMOTO in back. During the Cop's dialogue, Yamamoto appears to attempt harakiri and is prevented by another COP, who drags him out of the car and wrestles the knife away from him on the ground.

FAT COP
(as if to an off-camera reporter)

The Imperial Japanese School of Driving has been extremely successful in its designated purpose. With post-war immigration to Australia, Yamamoto and his team of instructor-fanatics have taught just about every new Australian, and the evidence of this is seen in our city streets every day. And on our footpaths, and trees and lampposts.

11   INT.   FILM COMMISSION OFFICE

SIR BRUCE and DOLLY stare at a small television set on which the FAT COP can be seen, gormlessly staring at nothing in particular.

Dolly switches it off.

> SIR BRUCE
> Positively inscrutable, these wily orientals.

> DOLLY
> Have you tried to scrute one, Sir Bruce?

> SIR BRUCE
> Not of late. One gets out of practice. Now, where is that clod Whipple we've been saddled with? I told him to be front and centre first thing in bright AM. And its half-past two. I'll be damned if I am going to make these early starts if my so-called staff can't keep pace with my dynamic business practices...

While he is speaking, Dolly tugs at his sleeve.

> DOLLY
> Sir Bruce...

> SIR BRUCE
> (cont'd)
> Where does one get reliable staff in the public service these days? Or any days?

Dolly continues to tug at his sleeve.

DOLLY

Sir Bruce...

SIR BRUCE
(cont'd)

Of course, the public service isn't what it used to be.
It used to be the East India Company until that
bugger Clive took to fancying yaks...

Dolly continues to tug at his sleeve.

DOLLY

Sir Bruce...

SIR BRUCE

Miss Mixture, will you please refrain from pecking
at me. Any moment, you will draw blood. Or loose
change.

DOLLY

There is someone here to see you.

SIR BRUCE

You never tell me anything, woman! I cannot
receive visitors unless I am behind my executive,
decision-making desk.

Sir Bruce rushes into his office. He passes the cupboard from
which MERVYN is trying to extricate himself. Sir Bruce slams
the door shut on Mervyn, and dashes into his office, slamming
the door closed.

DOLLY

(as Sir Bruce is leaving)

How can a desk make decisions? (To herself) A desk is an inanimate object. Without thought, self-will or ego. That's just plain silly.

She sits behind the desk and starts to unload her enormous handbag.

12   INT.   SIR BRUCE'S OFFICE

SIR BRUCE makes frenzied efforts to make the office presentable to visitors. He hides several empty whisky bottles and some pornographic magazines, moves all the papers from his 'In' tray to his 'Out' tray, grabs several film reference books from the waste bin and puts them on his desk.

He straightens on the wall an obviously fake photo of himself kissing Leonardo Caprio, checks the chair opposite his desk is lower than his. He sits down in his chair, which almost tilts him out backwards, grabs a copy of *Variety* and pretends to read it.

13   INT.   COMMISSION MAIN OFFICE

DOLLY hoovers her pot plants – the hose of the cleaner runs into her handbag as if the vacuum cleaner is in there. She looks up suddenly and with surprise.

REX PIRANHA stands in the front door, silhouetted against the light and flanked by TWO HUGE NUNS, wearing sidearms.

REX

Wait for me in the car, boys.

The two nuns look at each other, movie gangster-style.

Rex walks into the office, revealing behind him, a TINY NUN.

TINY NUN

Ok, you heard him, Sister Fang, Sister Toecutter. Go on, Gerroutofit!

SISTER FANG
(deep gruff voice)

Right, Mother Mate.

Tiny Nun pushes the other two out.

Dolly puts her glasses on and stares at Rex.

DOLLY

Hello, welcome and how may I lighten your little load?

REX

Come on, Dolly. I haven't changed much. Just my socks once a fortnight.

DOLLY

Heavens, it's Mr Piranha. I didn't recognise you with my glasses on.

REX

But I'm not wearing your glasses.

DOLLY

Somebody is. I'm a silly sausage sizzle. It's me. And
you're you. And you will want to see Sir Bruce. You
can borrow my glasses to see him with.

REX

Nobody in their right mind wants to see Bruce, but
I do need to speak with him.

Dolly flips then pages of an oversized diary.

DOLLY

Now let me have a little look-see. Do we have an
appointment at all?

REX

Strewth, Dolly. If people knew where I'd be ahead
of time, they could give Chopper Read a call.

DOLLY

I could probably squeeze you in now and Mister
Read later. I'll just have a tiny peep to see if Sir
Bruce is free.

Dolly flings open the door to Sir Bruce's office, and pokes her
head in.

DOLLY
(fishwife shriek)
Are you free, Sir Bruce?

14   INT.   SIR BRUCE'S OFFICE

SIR BRUCE falls off his chair in shock. He scrambles up, trying to pretend nothing happened.

> **SIR BRUCE**
> Good dogbolter, Miss Mixture. Of course I am not free. I make a small charge to cover overheads and underpants.

> **DOLLY**
> No. No. There's somebody here to see you.

> **SIR BRUCE**
> Sacre nodule! It's not the official auditor already? Tell him I am absent attending my own funeral, and send him to the clod Whipple.

> **DOLLY**
> Mercy me.   It's nothing like that. It's only Mr Piranha.

> **SIR BRUCE**
> Mon bleeding dieu, woman! That's worse. Don't just stand there. Go and check the petty cash tin at once. And lock up the tea spoons. And any virgins in the vicinity.

REX walks into the office.

> **REX**
> Same old Sir Bruce. Always an astute judge of character, for a man who has none of his own. I could never put one over on you.

DOLLY

What never?

REX

Well, hardly ever.

Sir Bruce comes around his desk and shakes Rex's hand, then suddenly snatches his hand a way and checks to see his watch is still on his wrist. He backs away behind his desk.

SIR BRUCE

Well, Rex, old mate. Take a seat. That is to say, sit down.

As Rex sits, Sir Bruce takes off his wristwatch, takes out his wallet and loose change and locks the lot in his desk drawer. He swallows the key.

REX

I hope I am not too late.

Rex rolls up his sleeve to reveal an armful of wristwatches.

REX

I don't suppose I could interest you in one of these little numbers. They fell out of the front of a jeweller's shop.

SIR BRUCE

Having you cluttering up my office and offering me goods of dodgy provenance takes me back, old son. Right back to when I was director of the Prevent Colleen McCullogh Fund.

REX

Right about the time I had the classic Vauxhall Viva, Hillman Imp and Ford Anglia dealership for Bullamakanka and the Southern Tablelands, I reckon.

DOLLY

Well, if you boys are going to start swapping grisly men's stories, I'll get on with my daily grind.

She leaves the office.

REX

As you know, since those days I have never looked back.

SIR BRUCE

Too bloody right. You wouldn't have dared. While you're here, I want to talk to you, Rex, about this company car tax-dodge lurk.

REX

Right up my alley.

SIR BRUCE

That's as may be, and I certainly am not following you up any murky passages. But the situation is simply that I cannot keep coming on the back of Miss Mixture's Lambretta. If nothing else, the foxtail on the aerial keeps blowing straight up my nose.

He sits down behind his desk, and is nearly thrown backwards out of his chair.

> REX
>
> I could see how that could be a bit of a problem.

> SIR BRUCE
>
> What could?

> REX
>
> About the fox.

> SIR BRUCE
>
> What fox?

> REX
>
> Yes.

> SIR BRUCE
>
> Oh.

> REX
>
> You mean, the car?

> SIR BRUCE
>
> What car?

> REX
>
> Yes.

> SIR BRUCE
>
> Oh.

While Sir Bruce and Rex stare at each blankly, Dolly comes back into the office.

> DOLLY
>
> Hello, you two. Sorry to interrupt your intense little chinwag. Sir Bruce, have you seen the foxtail off my aerial, perchance?

> SIR BRUCE
>
> What aerial?

> REX
>
> You mean, the car?

> DOLLY
>
> What car?

> REX
>
> Yes.

> SIR BRUCE
>
> Oh.

They all look blankly at each other.

MERVYN comes in.

> MERVYN
>
> Afternoon, Sir Bruce. Afternoon, everyone. Look what I just found next to the flushmatic. A little pussy-cat in one of your hankies, Sir Bruce.

Mervyn holds up a grubby handkerchief in which there is a curled-up fox tail.

                    SIR BRUCE
        Which hankie?

                    MERVYN
        This one. With the cat's tail just peeping out.

                    SIR BRUCE
        What cat's tail?

                    REX
        You mean, the car?

                    MERVYN
        Oh.

Dolly takes the fox tail out of the handkerchief. Mervyn drops the handkerchief with considerable distaste into the waste bin.

                    DOLLY
        This is just like the one of my aerial.

                    MERVYN
        What aerial?

                    REX
        You mean, the car?

                    SIR BRUCE
        No, the scooter.

                                    REX
You want to lease a scooter for tax purposes?

                                   DOLLY
It's a fox tail.

                                    REX
Even I can't get a foxtail on a tax concession.

                                   DOLLY
But you can get one on an aerial.

                                  MERVYN
You can get a tax concession on an aerial?

                                    REX
No, only on a car.

                                 SIR BRUCE
What car?

                                  MERVYN
The one with the aerial on it.

                                   DOLLY
My scooter has an aerial on it. Can I get a tax
concession on that?

                                    REX
Only if you have a car attached to it.

                                   DOLLY
It had a fox tail attached to it.

SIR BRUCE

What blasted car?

REX

Yes.

SIR BRUCE

Oh.

MERVYN

I don't wish to speak out of turn, Sir Bruce...

SIR BRUCE

Is it your turn?

Rex shrugs. Dolly starts to do an eeny-meeny-miney-mo count.

MERVYN

I think there is some merit in the notion of independent executive mobility.

All look at each other blankly.

MERVYN

Why doesn't the Commission get a car?

SIR BRUCE

Pon my soul, Whipple, you're not the idiot I took you for.

DOLLY

Oh, which idiot is he, Sir Bruce?

SIR BRUCE

After due consideration, it strikes me that an official
Commission car would save me having to come to
meetings on Miss Mixture's Lambretta and prevent,
and let me make this perfect clear, prevent her fox
tail getting up my nasal orifices.

DOLLY

But I've lost my little fox tail.

MERVYN

Why don't you have the one I just found?

DOLLY

How sweet. It's just like the one I used to have.

REX

Now look here, Sir Bruce. I am in a position to do
you a bit of good.

Sir Bruce stands up from behind his desk and looks down at Rex
(who is out of shot on the floor).

SIR BRUCE

Good god, Rex. So you are! (Pause) I didn't know
you could do calisthenics.

Rex struggles up from the floor. Sir Bruce sits back into his chair
with the usual consequence.

REX

If we could just get rid of the crowd in here, we can
talk this one through.

SIR BRUCE

I'm with you, Rex. If you could just excuse us, Miss Mixture.

DOLLY

You're excused. (Sniffs) What did you do, Sir Bruce?

SIR BRUCE

What? No. Rex and I need to thrash this thing out between us. Alone.

Dolly and Mervyn nod in agreement but actually without comprehension.

SIR BRUCE

We require to be sequestered to contemplate its ramifications.

Dolly and Mervyn continue to stand there and nod vacantly.

SIR BRUCE

Privately. Just Rex. And me. In this office. By ourselves. Alone.

Nodding but no move to leave.

SIR BRUCE

We require, and let me make this perfectly clear, seclusion. Solitude. Confinement.

Dolly starts taking notes.

SIR BRUCE

Not to put too fine a point on it, therefore, that door behind you should become in effect a purdah, a barrier designed to ensure that which takes place behind it remains hidden, an obstacle between Rex and myself on one side and you on the other. This will be achieved by both of you stepping across the threshold and closing the door, from the outside. Thus rendering us bereft of your presence.

Dolly takes all this down in shorthand. Mervyn pays rapt attention. Neither attempt to leave.

REX

Oh for gawd's sake. Piss off the pair of you, or I'll drop you.

Dolly and Mervyn scurry out at speed.

15   INT.   COMMISSION MAIN OFFICE

DOLLY sits down at her desk and pulls out a ten-metre length of knitting from her bag.

DOLLY
(sheepishly)
I can never remember how to turn the corner when knitting socks. (Sighs)

MERVYN
Who is this fellow, Mr Piranha? I must say he seemed well acquainted with your little foibles.

DOLLY

What these?

She places her hands inside her blouse and fiddles around for a while. She pulls out a string of pearls.

DOLLY

Aren't they nice? Rex bought them at Foible and Gibson, before they were taken over by Earl Grey.

MERVYN

My finely-honed public service paranoia tells me he seems a strange sort of confidante for someone in Sir Bruce's position.

DOLLY

Oh, Sir Bruce is capable of a number of interesting positions for a man of his stature. Rex has been in on everything Sir Bruce has been up to since the beginning. (Pause) He never seems to be around at the end though. Maybe I'll just pop outside and make a note of his getaway car registration number. You never know.

She winds the knitting around Mervyn's head and neck, and goes out the front door.

16   EXT.   FRONT OF COMMISSION OFFICE

DOLLY comes out of the front door and starts peering up and down the street. ROY CLEGHORN climbs awkwardly backwards out of a badly parked, battered LANDROVER, and collides with Dolly. Roy is trying to keep a (unseen) creature in the car.

194

ROY

Careful where you stick your decolletage, lady, when a bloke's backing up.

DOLLY

A man of your age ought to know better than to get out of the passenger side without looking.

ROY

I wouldn't have had to if that bloody kangaroo hadn't insisting on driving.

The creature thumps and crashes about inside the car.

WIMPEY
(off)

Tch. Tch. Tch.

ROY

I'm not going to continue this discuss if you can't argue rationally.

DOLLY

Well I never. I was just stating a well-known fact.

ROY

No, I wasn't talking to you. I was talking to him.

WIMPEY
(off)

Tch. Tch. Tch.

ROY

I don't bloody care what Rousseau may or may not have said about the existence of god, you're not getting out of this car.

WIMPEY
(off)

Tch. Tch. Tch.

ROY

No, it's bad enough you talked me into letting you drive when you only have a licence for automatics.

He slams the door.

ROY

Can you point me in the direction of the Rottnest Island Film Commission, girly?

DOLLY

It's right in front of your nose, boysie.

Roy pulls out a map and compass from his commodious Bombay Bloomers.

ROY
(mutters)

That's me moustache, right in front of me nose. It might have a few boogies stuck in it, but it's still me mo.

He walks off down the street, holding his compass out in front.

WIMPEY
(off)

Tch. Tch. Tch.

DOLLY

Just stop that silly nonsense. Everyone knows that
Descartes was a better philosopher than Hegel.

She goes back inside the office.

17   INT.   MAIN OFFICE

MERVYN sits at his own desk, counting beans from a large jar.

SIR BRUCE enters from his own office, sees Mervyn, and turns
back to look at REX.

SIR BRUCE
(to Rex)
You were quite right, Rex. He is a little, jumped-up
bean counter.

DOLLY comes in from outside.

SIR BRUCE
Ah, Miss Mixture, take a letter.

DOLLY
Oh, er, Que. Did I get it right? Such a clever party
trick. It never gets stale.

SIR BRUCE
What on earth are you rambling about? Take these
down at once.

DOLLY
Oh, Sir Bruce. I didn't know you cared.

SIR BRUCE

Frankly, my dear, I don't give damn. But I won't have panty hose hanging all around the office.

Dolly starts to take down a pair of panty hose pegged to a line across one corner of the office.

DOLLY

How is a working girl supposed to keep her smalls in good order and condition. It's that greasy Lambretta.

SIR BRUCE

What you do with persons of Southern Mediterranean extraction is between you and the bedpost, Miss Mixture. Now, if I could prevail upon you to sit yourself and try on a minor memo?

DOLLY

But of course, Sir Bruce. Why didn't you say in the first place? The skidmarks on my underwear are not so important they couldn't wait.

Dolly sits at her desk, turns on her PC, puts on her glasses, stretches and cracks her knuckles and stares at the screen as if she could cause it to function by sheer willpower.

DOLLY

Okey dokes.

                         SIR BRUCE
A memo to Finklestein, Finklestein, Finklestein and
Wong, Theatrical agents and camel traders, Cairo,
Egypt, Africa, Northern Hemisphere, the World,
the Milky Way, the Universe. Begin it, Dear
Darryl...

Dolly makes a few taps at the keyboard.

                         SIR BRUCE
Re yours of the fourteen ultimatum, vis-a-vis, ipso
facto, therefore, notwithstanding, wherein we have
heretofore and without prejudice to a priori
arrangements notwithstanding and inasmuch as we
have without malice aforethought contracted
through and on behalf of the Rottnest Island Film
Commission, hereinafter known as the Commission
and the party of the first part of the party, and your
good selves, hereinafter yourselves and the party of
the second part of the party, on behalf of and
without obligation, prejudice, predetermination or
giving a flying fart, to and/or against Miss Tequila
Mockingbird, the party of the third party of the
party who will, upon completion of this contract,
become the party of the second part of the party.
Can Miss Mockingbird start work on Monday?
Remind her to bring a cut lunch.

Dolly types for a split second.

                          DOLLY
Cut lunch. Got that, Sir Bruce.

SIR BRUCE

Sign that, Sir Bruce.

Dolly types for a long time.

DOLLY

Is that it?

A printer spews out a sheet of paper, which Dolly hands to Sir Bruce. He signs it with a quill pen, dipped in ink, from Dolly's desk. She blots it with a handful of sand from her handbag.

As this is happening, SOUNDS OFF: KOOKABURRA and HOBNAIL BOOTS.

ROY
(off)
Coo-bloody-ee, Cobblers!

Sir Bruce, Dolly and Mervyn turn to look at the front door.

SOUND: body falling downstairs
SOUND: A kookaburra being sat on.

ROY
(off)

Ah, shifting sands.

All stare at the still unseen Roy.

SIR BRUCE

Who is this clod? Does anyone know? Does anyone care? See him off the premises, Whipple.

MERVYN

No. This clod, Sir Bruce, is Roy Clodhorn, er, sorry, I mean Roy Cleghorn, noted bushwalker and camper.

SIR BRUCE

He can't camp here. You are quite camp enough for a commission of this size.

ROY
(off)

Cripes, I've landed fair on me burra.

MERVYN

Mr Cleghorn trained the wombat stampede in Picnic at Hanging Rock.

DOLLY

But I have seen Picnic at Hanging Rock oh so many times. There was no wombat stampede, was there, Sir Bruce?

SIR BRUCE

How would I know? I never go to the cinema.

ROY
(off)

The bludgers cut it out. Why'd you reckon we never find out what happened to them sheilas in the nighties?

Sir Bruce takes Mervyn to one side.

Through the open door to Sir Bruce's office, REX can be seen trying to unscrew a painting from the wall and when that fails, taking a pocket knife and cutting it out of the frame and putting it under his coat.

                    SIR BRUCE
          What's on the go here, Whipple. Is this some
          devious plot by my enemies in high places? Or low
          places? Or any places?

                    MERVYN
          Roy Cleghorn is part of the conditions under which
          we were given the grant for that ecological film
          project, The Wombat That Ate Ayres Rock.

                    SIR BRUCE
          Let me get this perfectly clear. You mean that in
          return for that massive, non-repayable, government
          grant, we have been stuck with this massive non-
          returnable idiot?

                    MERVYN
          In a word, and to put it simply, to avoid confusion,
          and   in   order   to   obviate   any   possible
          miscomprehension - yes.

                    SIR BRUCE
          Oh.

ROY walks in with his foot stuck in a bucket and holding an extremely flat kookaburra, shedding feathers. He kicks the bucket off and it crashes against the wall.

BERT scurries out from the far recesses of the office and picks up the bucket which he strokes soothingly.

> ROY
>
> G'day Merve. Cripes I just come a real gutsa on top of me burra. What flaming mongrel left that bucket at the top of the stairs?

> BERT
>
> It's all right for you, matey. But this bucket's father died in the war for people like you.

18   EXT. LOCATION AS IN EXECUTION IN *BREAKER MORANT* DAY

A BUCKET is brought out by a squad of SOLDIERS, placed on a chair, blindfolded and shot by a FIRING SQUAD.

19   INT.   MAIN OFFICE

> BERT wanders off to his dark hole, holding the bucket like a sick baby.

> BERT
>
> It's bad enough having Lambretta brake fluid mixed up with a man's Handy Andy, but having to get mashed kookaburra out of the grouting is where I draw the line. Me old Granddad used to say, 'Son, you can always stone the crows, but don't ever, don't never, sit on a kookaburra. They've got ruddy sharp peckers.'

A LITTLE OLD MAN, an ancient version of Bert, steps out of a cupboard.

GRANDDAD

Never did. What I said was 'Never get a kooka's pecker up your clacker'.

BERT

Oh shut up.

He picks Granddad up and hurls him out the back window.

MERVYN
(to Roy)

I'd like you to meet the Chairman of the Commission. Sir Bruce, Roy.

ROY

G'day, Brucie. I met your brother in India after the mutiny, Viceroy.

Roy shakes Sir Bruce's hand in an overwhelmingly hearty fashion.

SIR BRUCE

Oh, really?

ROY

Say, Brucie, who's the bonza looking bit of skirt with the legs like a bungarra.

SIR BRUCE

How does that go in English?

ROY

That bit of all right with the expression of a startled dugong.

SIR BRUCE

I can only surmise that you are referring to Miss Mixture, my Girl Friday.

ROY

Cripes, am I in the wrong possie. One for every day of the week, eh? How about overtime on Sundays, eh?

Dolly has been polishing pot plants with Brasso. She walks up to Sir Bruce.

SIR BRUCE

Miss Mixture, I think I would like you to meet Roy, er...

Roy grasps Dolly's hand and shakes it vigorous. As she is holding a tin of Brasso, it flies all over the place.

ROY

Cleghorn. Cleghorn by name and Cleghorn by inclination.

DOLLY

Are you the Roy Cleghorn my mother told me climbed up the Three Sisters?

ROY

Wombats, that's me all right. As I always say, it's
harder getting up the Three Sisters than down.

DOLLY

That's nice.

SIR BRUCE

Oh, really?

ROY

Enough beating around the back blocks. Cop this,
Brucie. I'm fair chockers with bonza ideas for some
fair dinkum films.

A silent, tense moment follows while all work out what Roy has
just said. Then all, including, Bert, commencing pounding the
crap out of him.

ANGLE

ARLENE FARQUHAR, holding a microphone, walks into shot
and addresses the camera.

ARLENE

Roy Cleghorn. Man or myth? Or merely a legend in
his own lunch box? It's time the lid was ripped off
that lunch box. Tonight, on 'Roy Cleghorn: This is
Your Fault', we will completely lose sight of the
truth in order to make the sort of crapulous
television that gets ratings, attracts sponsors and
keeps me in gainful employment.

20   EXT.   TYPICAL AUSTRALIAN SUBURBAN HOME

KERRY O'BRIEN, hair suspiciously redder than usual, stands outside the house.   His expression turns from vacant gormlessness to intensity.

> KERRY
> It was in this house or one very much like it, that Roy Cleghorn was thought up by the writers of this series. In fact, it was not in the house at all. This is, in truth, my mother's house. And I am going inside to see if I can't make contact – and perhaps get a cup of tea.

21   INT.   KERRY'S MOTHER'S HOUSE

KERRY walks down the corridor towards the camera.

> KERRY
> If we keep quiet, and listen carefully, we might just hear the dulcet sounds of my mother and her sisters, my aunts, in the time-honoured ritual of afternoon tea.

SOUNDS OFF: Raucous, screaming female voices, crashing of crockery, belching and farting, a pneumatic drill, a kookaburra being sat on.

22   INT.   KERRY'S MOTHER'S KITCHEN DAY

A Crowd of ELDERLY WOMEN sit around the table, deep in meaningless conversation, lamingtons, tea pots, crockery, crocheting, and so on.

KERRY enters and sits at the table.

> KERRY
> (To camera)
> Now if I sit quietly and try not to frighten these sensitive and peaceful creatures...

TWO AUNTS begin beating each over the head with household implements.

> KERRY
> (Cont'd)
> ...we may gain a real insight into the structure of their surprisingly sophisticated society.

> AN AUNT
> ... and if you think getting dog vomit out of the Axminster is hard, you should try and get mashed kookaburra out of the grouting.

> KERRY'S MOTHER
> There you are at last, love. Have you washed you hands? Now shut up and suck your tea, there's a good boy.

KERRY'S MOTHER places a cup of tea in front of him and ties a Peter Rabbit bib around his neck. She takes his microphone and addresses the camera.

> KERRY'S MOTHER
> Curious and fascinating as the consumption of iced vo-vos may be amongst these striking creatures, there are aspects of the suburban male that bear investigation.

She leaves the kitchen, then pops her head back in.

>   KERRY'S MOTHER
>   (To camera crew)
>   Are you coming or not?

>   AN AUNT
>   Where's Myrtle off to then?

>   ANOTHER AUNT
>   She always was flighty. (To Kerry) That's why she
>   married your father. He was in the Luftwaffe – by
>   mistake. Now open wide.

She pushes a whole lamington into Kerry's mouth.

23   EXT.   SUBURBAN BACKYARD

Smoke pours out of windows, eaves and holes in A LARGE
GARDEN SHED.

>   KERRY'S MOTHER
>   Wolfgang! Wolfie! He's always pottering about in
>   there somewhere.
>   (To camera)
>   It was this man, or one very much like him, who was
>   Kerry's father. (Pause) Or was he Roy's father?

In a great cloud of smoke, KERRY's FATHER comes out of the
shed.

SOUND OFF: Like a chicken strangling.

KERRY'S MOTHER

Ooh-er. That was either the kettle boiling or one of
Kerry's aunties being sick.

She hands the microphone to Kerry's Father and rushes off.

KERRY'S FATHER

I first met Roy Cleghorn in Darwin during the war
when he was up to his elbows in evacuating
buffaloes. Naturally we did not get very close. I
have never seen him since, thank the lord. I wonder
what he is doing now?

24   INT.   COMMISSION MAIN OFFICE

ARLENE bandages ROY's head.

ARLENE
(To camera)
It is difficult to believe that this tattered wreck of a
man, woman and spinster of this parish is
responsible for teaching the Leyland Brothers, Les
Hiddins and Albie Mangles all they know, and a few
things they don't, about negotiating lucrative media
contracts.

25   EXT.   AUSTRALIAN DESERT

ROY shows LES HIDDINS how to catch a goanna. Through
elaborate mime, he picks up a goanna, hits it on the head with a
large mallet, stuffs it under a rock. He then feigns stealth,
surprise and capture. He gets Les to do the same. The goanna
bites Les.

26   INT.   FILM EDITING SUITE

Earnest but scruffy type turns away from editing desk to face the camera.

CAPTION: Peter Weird Film Director.

> WEIRD
> I first became aware of Roy Cleghorn's unique rapport with animals when we worked together on the Skippy series...

ANGLE: Zoom in to frame held on editor viewer which becomes...

27   EXT.   BUSH LOCATION

ROY stands over a (stuffed) WALLABY, pointing a shotgun at its head and gesticulating. The wallaby does not move. Roy leaps up and down, and shouts at it. Eventually he blows it to bits. TWO MEN carry on a box marked 'Skippies. Fragile. This Way Up'. They reach in and bring out another (stuffed) wallaby. Roy reloads the gun and starts pointing and shouting.

ANGLE
Zoom out, and shot becomes the shot in the viewer in...

28   INT.   FILM EDITING SUITE

Before it gets too small, Roy blows the second wallaby to bits.

WEIRD

It is easy to see why I immediately thought of Roy Cleghorn when I came to make Barbecue at Hanging Rock, and I had a whole batch of pubescent school girls to whip into line.

29   INT.   COMMISSION MAIN OFFICE

ARLENE addresses the camera. Behind her, REX, opens a jeroboam of champagne, and pours it for SIR BRUCE, DOLLY, MERVYN and ROY.

ARLENE

This then is the man in whom the Rottnest Island Film Commission invests its future, and a great deal of our money. But is an over-familiarity with furry marsupials and other aspects of the flora and fauna of this great country of ours sufficient grounds for the confidence which this great country of ours has thus expressed? Only time will tell whether there lurks beneath those baggy Bombay Bloomers a rampart and thrusting desire for Australian bush creatures, to put furry things on the cinema screen of the world. Only time and the RSPCA will tell. This is Arlene Farquhar for 'This Is Your Fault'. Goodnight.

ANGLE

As she speaks, the camera moves around from in front of her to join the others in the background. It finishes up looking at her from behind, revealing she is talking to a blank wall. The others make signs to each other that she is potty.

END CREDIT
MUSIC OVER

Arlene turns and walks to others, obviously shouting about being left talking to a wall. Others josh her.

FADE OUT

END CREDITS

> SIR BRUCE
> (Over)
> Rex, old lad, you wouldn't sell me a lemon, would you?

> REX
> (Over)
> You'll have to suck it and see.

30   EXT.   A USED CAR YARD

SIR BRUCE stands up from between two rows of cars. He wipes his mouth.

> SIR BRUCE
> Do you have these commodores in another flavour?

CREDITS CONTINUE

END OF EPISODE

It became necessary, when submitting television material to the stony gaze of television executives, producers and other forms of pond life, to slightly modify the Character Descriptions that had previously been written to support radio episodes. The demands of working (as Lyon and Rattigan would have wished to do) in a visual medium meant that some sense of the appearance of the characters needed to be made and, at the same time, a requirement to downplay the attempt to be simply comic rather than 'professional'. The description of characters that accompanied the television script is reproduced below.

MAIN CHARACTERS

The main characters of the Rottnest Island Film Commission are either the members of the Board of Directors of the Commission, or its employees.

Other regular characters are a television broadcaster who appears at particular moments to comment, televisually, on events or characters; an aged cleaner that the Commission has inherited along with its premises; and a gargantuan tea-lady.

CHAIRMAN OF THE BOARD OF DIRECTORS: SIR BRUCE FERNARGLE-JONES.

An imposing figure, not unlike ex-Prime Minister Gough Whitlam in both physical appearance and manner of speech. Sir Bruce is tall, with grey hair and thick eyebrows. He has a ruddy complexion suggesting frequent imbibing, and a plump appearance suggesting frequent dining as well. A bluff, occasionally gruff, figure of fairly limited intelligence, but with a reasonably acute eye for the main chance. Sir Bruce has a penchant for pedantry but tends to retreat rapidly (if not run away entirely) when his bluff is called.

MEMBERS OF THE BOARD OF DIRECTORS:

REX 'SLICK' PIRANHA.
A man of indeterminate middle-age who always dresses loudly and younger than his years. He wears his thinning hair longer than necessary, and slicks it down with hair-oil. Like Sir Bruce, Rex knows nothing about films, but he is aware of every tax dodge and loophole going. He has contacts with many shady organizations and is usually only one step ahead of the law, and two steps ahead of the members of the organizations he has business dealings with. He brings to the Commission a business acumen honed by many years of dealing in used cars.

ROY CLEGHORN.
The quintessential Australian bushman: short, brown, wrinkled by the sun, with knock-knees. He wears Bombay bloomer shorts and a broad-brimmed hat trimmed in mouldy animal fur. Roy is much given to expressions of an ecological nature (most of them variants of 'stone the crows'). He is between forty and fifty years of age. He speaks with a very distinct Australian drawl and is slightly out of his depth in the high-pressure world of film production.

EMPLOYEES OF THE ROTTNEST FILM COMMISSION

MERVYN WHIPPLE
A slim, precise, slightly camp figure. Mervyn is in his early thirties and a career public servant. He dresses in conservative suits, is bespectacled, slightly balding and is never without his furled umbrella and synthetic crocodile-skin briefcase. A born worrier, he perceives loyalty to the Public Service in general is more important than loyalty to any particular department or chief but is prepared to make the most of every opportunity for promotion. His particular nemesis at the Rottnest Island Film Commission is not the Chairman but the bucket that belongs to Bert the cleaner.

215

DOLLY MIXTURE: SECRETARY TO THE CHAIRMAN

A spinster of more than mature years, Dolly still has not given up hope. Smallish but well-dressed (in an inevitable variation of twin-set and pearls), Dolly manages bouffant hair-do that frequently threatens to collapse, and make-up that frequently threatens to crack and erode. After a lifetime of secretarial positions, many with Sir Bruce Fernargle-Jones, Dolly has accumulated a number of essential possessions which she carries everywhere with her – in a large, seemingly bottomless handbag. Dolly has a habit of clutching her pearls close to her throat when she hears or sees something distasteful.

OTHERS:

BERT

Nobody knows Bert's last name or even if he has one. Bert is not actually an employee of the Rottnest Island Film Commission. When the Commission moved into its new premises, Bert was already in attendance as a cleaner, carrying on a noble family tradition. Bert refuses to leave and is generally ignored by everyone. As near as can be ascertained from his incessant mumbling, Bert has served King and/or Queen and Country in every war since the Crimea and is fully confident of serving in the next one.

GLADYS TULE

Gladys has a roving commission as public service tea-woman-at-large. The job description is particularly apt as Gladys is of such physical dimensions as to cause passing Sumo wrestlers to faint with envy. Beneath the acres of her ample bosom beats, with considerable difficulty, a heart of gold. She has a particular soft spot for Bert.

ARLENE FARQUHAR

Arlene appears at occasional moments in the programmes, usually when there is something of national importance that needs to be commented upon via television. She is an enthusiastic young woman who wears 'grasshopper eye' style spectacles and usually has her blonde hair tied back in severe fashion. Her role varies from straight newsreader to on-the-spot reporter to anchor-person for current affairs programmes, depending on the demands of the situation.

Rejection 2.0

BROADCAST HOUSE 145-153 ELIZABETH STREET SYDNEY 2000 TELEPHONE (02) 339 0211

AUSTRALIAN BROADCASTING CORPORATION

Head Office

20 November 1984

Mr Neil Rattigan
24 Wattle Street
SOUTH PERTH WA 6151

Dear Mr Rattigan

It's not often I read scripts which make me laugh and parts of yours did.
That makes a rejection letter a lot harder to write and, I suppose, to read.

The main problem seems to be that you're writing with an all-film bias when
television, our sort of television anyway, is largely electronic.

We make situation comedy which, by universal definition, is tightly written
for two or three sets, uses a small cast, a very small percentage of location
recording and is designed for production in front of a studio audience much
like a stage play. Even worse, production needs to be completed inside a
two hour period!

Obviously, it's a highly specialised area and it places enormous restrictions
on a writer forcing him to write character and character conflict rather than
action. Special effects, because of the time they take and the difficulty
involved in bringing them off in front of an audience are usually avoided.
The best advice I can give you is to quote Paddy Chayefski who always told
aspiring television writers to "Think small".

But you do make me laugh and I think you'd make other people laugh as well.
If you could just bridle the imagination a bit and force yourself to
concentrate on the character relationships maybe we'll eventually be able
to do business.

At the moment, both your proposals are far too big for us not only in terms
of production style but because they'd need budgets that wouldn't disgrace
a feature film.

Don't go away. I'd like to see something I could afford to make. Any
questions?

Sincerely

JOHN O'GRADY
Executive Producer
TV Entertainment

POSTAL ADDRESS GPO BOX 9994 SYDNEY NSW 2001 TELEX 20323 · INTERNATIONAL TELEX 28506
Television Studios — Pacific Highway Gore Hill Telephone (02) 437 8000
Radio Studios — William Street/Upper Forbes Street Sydney Telephone (02) 339 0211

CHANNEL FOUR TELEVISION 60 CHARLOTTE STREET, LONDON W1P 2AX. TELEPHONE: 01 631 4444. TELEX: 892355

3rd October, 1985

Neil Rattigan,
London House,
Mecklenburgh Square,
London WC1N 2AB

Dear Neil,

Many thanks for sending me ROTTNEST ISLAND FILM COMMISSION and
FUNNY FARM. I enjoyed reading both scripts immensely, but I am
afraid that we won't be able to proceed with them.

ROTTNEST ISLAND had a great deal of humour and I enjoyed the
wonderfully unlikely characters that you create, like Dolly Mixture
and Rex Piranha. However, I am not convinced that anybody is going
to be interested in a comedy series set in a film commissioning
body - believe me, life in this commissioning unit is not FUNNY!

FUNNY FARM, I felt, was extremely intelligent, but I am afraid it was
too Australian for us to make it in this country.

I am sorry to disappoint you, but at a time when funds are tight we
really have to concentrate on our priorities. I would be very
happy to read any more of your scripts that you might have to send
in six months or so, when it is conceivable that we might have more
money to spend.

Best wishes,

Seamus Cassidy
Assistant Commissioning Editor, Light Entertainment

CHANNEL FOUR TELEVISION COMPANY LIMITED
REGISTERED IN CARDIFF UNDER NO. 1533774. REGISTERED OFFICE: 70 BROMPTON ROAD, LONDON SW3 1RY.
THE RT. HON. R. J. LUND DELL (CHAIRMAN), SIR RICHARD ATTENBOROUGH (DEPUTY CHAIRMAN), JEREMY ISAACS (CHIEF EXECUTIVE),
JUSTIN DUKES (MANAGING DIRECTOR), PAUL BONNER, SIR BRIAN BAILEY, LORD BLAKE, CARMEN CALLIL, PAUL FOX, JAMES GATWARD,
JOHN GAU, DETTA O'CATHAIN, ANTHONY PRAGNELL, PETER ROGERS, MICHAEL SCOTT, DR. GLYN TEGAI HUGHES.

220

At various times and in a mood of outrage, Sir Bruce felt obliged to defend the reputation of the Rottnest Island Film Commission.

The following copies are of letters that have been rescued from the ravages of silver fish.

Although undated the first of these seems self-evidently to have been written in 1980. It is not known if the letter was printed in the Sunday Independent. The date of the second is not noted. However, it seems it may have been written and sent during the time that Sir Bruce was broadcasting on the ABC in the early 1990s. As far as is known the Verity James to whom the letter was addressed was a presenter and/or producer on ABC radio in Perth (and clearly, as the letter implies, ought to have known better).

ROTTNEST ISLAND FILM COMMISSION

Protect Australia's Image: Tell Lies

The Editor,
Sunday Independent,
7 Briggs Street,
EAST VICTORIA PARK, W.A. 6101

Dear Sir and/or Madam,

We at the Rottnest Island Film Commission wish to register the strongest possible objection to the slur made on the reputation of our Subsidiary Entrepreneurial Enterprise (S.E.E.) of the Rottnest Cinema which appeared on page 68 of your disreputable rag on January 20th 1980.

We refer, of course, to the suggestion by the pseudonymous 'Eye-spy' that the film 'CYBORG 2087' would be rejected by 'even' the Rottnest Cinema. Not only does this remark suggest that the Rottnest Cinema perpetuates a tradition of screening less than internationally acclaimed award winning films but the claim is also untrue. 'CYBORG 2087' recently enjoyed a record breaking season at the Rottnest Island Cinema (S.E.E. - see!) and was also awarded the Gold Claw by a panel of independent Quokkas.

Further, it should be pointed out that the second assistant clapper loader for this film was Mr. Mustapha Kupatea, a Turkish citizen who, pending a visa from the immigration department and health clearance, has accepted a consultative position with the Rottnest Island Film Commission.

One of the first tasks Mustapha will undertake, on commencing his employment with the Rottnest Island Film Commission, will be to commence pre-production on 'CYBORG 2087 II, the Motion Picture

Sequel of the Same Name only Different by a Little Bit than the Other One' to be shot on location at Rottnest (depending upon a huge influx of immense Government Grants of a non-repayable nature).

In conclusion should this type of slur re-occur, we will find it necessary to send our Mr. Sockett Toomey to interview you over the head with a brick.

Very best wishes for 1980.

Yours faithfully,
Bruce
SIR BRUCE FERNARGLE-JONES
Chairman: Rottnest Island Film Commission

ROTTNEST ISLAND FILM COMMISSION

Protect Australia's Image: Tell Lies

Dear Verity James (if that really is your name),

We were appalled at the singular lack of interest your programme on the Western Australian film industry demonstrated toward the Rottnest Island Film Commission's activities.

The Rottnest Island Film Commission is an entrepreneurial body of the island government. A huge profit orientated organisation, its primal aim is to develop a stable but lucrative film-making industry on Rottnest Island.

In terms of operation it upholds the highest artistic and business standards, in order to present Australia flatteringly, particularly in the context of Rottnest Island, through documentary and especially fictional productions, at some future date.

The roles of the Rottnest Island Film Commission are to produce, market, distribute, exhibit and sell award-winning, internationally acclaimed films for the entertainment and education of adults, children, Aborigines and Vietnamese and to encourage aspiring and especially inexperienced newcomers to the film industry.

The Commission welcomes immense Government grants but has the right to borrow unlimited funds from any source using the Island Government treasury as guarantor and without expectation of profit from any of its entrepreneurial activities.

The Commission seeks to exploit the rich potential of the indigenous, dark-hued population and offers unprecedented incentives for feature length script concepts on leprosy, tourism, genocide, abalone diving, cannibalism, dysentery, nice scenery, scared sites and/or hotel extensions.

Please find attached brief professional backgrounds on Commission members. If you continue to ignore us and our efforts we may have to come 'round and interview you over the head with a brick.

Yours, till the cows come home to roost.

Bruce
Sir Bruce Fernargle-Jones: Chairperson and Treasurer

P.S. Thank your mother for the rabbits.

The following material was found in a manila file stuffed down the back of the rusty filing cabinet that constitutes the final resting place of the records of the Rottnest Island Film Commission. The inaccessibility of this material, presumably done intentionally, may explain why it was not confiscated by the relevant and/or irrelevant authorities or simply set fire to.

From the tenor of the contents of these pages it would seem that Lyon and Rattigan, recognising the growing unlikelihood of selling their Rottnest Island Film Commission scripts, attempted to sell themselves at journeymen humourists.

If so, that didn't work either.

ROTTNEST ISLAND FILM COMMISSION

Protect Australia's Image: Tell Lies

9th February 1981

Mr. John Sturzaker,
Program Development Manager,
Channel Seven,
Mobbs Lane,
EPPING, N.S.W. 2121

Dear John Sturzaker (or whatever your name really is),

We were devastated to read of the singular lack of success of the new comedy segment of the Willesee show. We cannot help but feel that it is all our fault as we did not respond to your advert of last year and offer our inestimable services to you.

Actually, it is all the fault of the silly ~~Old Cow~~ old age pensioner Bertha Tule, whom we allow to add to her miserable pension by earning a few bob typing letters for us. She insisted on going into hospital at that crucial moment for open-heart surgery. This was fair enough but when that was over she claimed to be unable to accommodate a typewriter in her oxygen tent and in any case the iron lung was plugged into the only available power point.

Equally, we didn't know what your advertisement really meant but it sounds like it's the very thing for us – as people claim that they don't know what we mean either. The meeting of two meaningless systems (outside the Houses of Parliament, of course) seems a phenomenon too replete with possibilities to be ignored. (With us so far?)

Seriously though, you need us like Hitler needed Stalingrad (historical joke), Orson Welles needed Perrier (obscure advertising joke), The Quoon needs Prince Phillip (Royalty joke) and we need spelling lessons (literacy joke).

Jokes aside, we have a proven track record, but since the greyhound died, we thought we'd write to you. We enclose copies of references and testimonies.

A telegram saying 'The job's yours, boys' will suffice.

Yours,

Neil and Bill

NEIL RATTIGAN and BILL LYON

PS   Is Mike Willesee really dead or does he just look that way?

PPS   Is a receding hairline an essential for working in television? If so, we are OK on that score.

PPPS We would have written more but we had already sealed the envelope - extremely old joke.

Encs

ROTTNEST ISLAND FILM COMMISSION

Protect Australia's Image: Tell Lies

From the desk of Sir Bruce Fernargle-Jones

TO WHOM IT MAY CONCERN

It gives me absolutely no pleasure (but the doctor is giving me something for it) to provide this reference for 'Thingy' and 'What's-his-name'.

Since being foisted upon us as part of a deal by which we acquired an immense unspecified, non-repayable government grant these two have amassed a <u>remarkable</u> list of credits.

They were largely responsible for the mass dysentery scene in Wayne Bertolucci's unreleased masterpiece *Ringrazia Loro Madre Per I Conigli.*

They also have contributed the following screenplays to internationally acclaimed, award winning Rottnest Island Film Commission productions:

King Quokka – an expose of nature's primitive lustful drives.

Quokkablanca – the love of a man, a woman and a piano-playing marsupial.

The Sound of Mucus – the first all diseased musical.

The Wombat That Ate Ayres Rock.

They also contributed to the following classics of adolescent cinema:

Gidget Has Menopause
Heidi Gets Stuffed
Tammy Gets Leprosy

And the definitive examination of Australia's role in the Vietnam war:
Aquokkalips Now

They are also responsible for that brilliant promotional campaign:
'You'll Believe A Man Can Fart Out His Ear!' *Ernie Crun – the Movie.*

As further tribute to their unbelievable, incomprehensible standing, sitting and lying in the cinematic community, here are some remarks from famous persons of the filmic firmament:

'I wouldn't be seen dead in one of their lousy movies ...' J. WAYNE
'Nor me!' - S. McQUEEN
'Bill and Neil who?' – H.R.H. THE QUOON
'Sorry y'all. Cannot appear in Rottnest Island Film for at least next four years'. – R. REAGAN

I would dearly like to see these lads go far as possible as soon as possible, please.

Warm regards to you and yours.

Bruce
Sir Bruce Fernargle-Jones OBE and Barred

ROTTNEST ISLAND FILM COMMISSION

Protect Australia's Image: Tell Lies

MEMORANDUM

TO: Sir Bruce Fernargle-Jones
FROM: Mervin Whipple, Personal Assistant to the Chairperson
SUBJECT: Reference for Lyon and Rattigan

Dear Sir Bruce,

Here's a god-sent opportunity to get rid of these two clods while there's a little of the non-specific grant money we use to pay them left.

Knock up a reference that makes them look good.

Don't worry, you can't be held legally liable for the lies you'll have to tell.

Cheers,

Mervyn
Mervin Whipple

P.S. Thank your mother for the rabbits.

16th February, 1981.

Messrs. Neil Rattigan and Bill Lyon,
24 Wattle Street,
South Perth, W.A., 6151.

Dear Neil and Bill,

Thank you very much for your recent letter to John
Sturzaker which has been passed on to us as we were
looking for writers etc. for our new show WILLESEE 81.

We have enough writers for the moment but we will
keep your letter on file for possible future
consideration.

Many thanks for contacting us.

Yours sincerely,

Michael Willesee

Michael Willesee.

Television Centre, Mobbs Lane, Epping, N.S.W. 2121 P.O. Box 216, Eastwood, N.S.W. 2122
Tel: 858 3388 Telex: WILOTV-AA27835

AFTERWORD

All funny fellows, comic men, and clowns of private life –
They'd none of them be missed – they'd none of them be missed.

W.S. Gilbert
'Little List' song, Act 1, *The Mikado* (1895)

And so it has turned out, O Best Beloved, that the once dynamic writing duo of Lyon and Rattigan has become no more than an insignificant dust-bunny beneath the Bedstead of History that doubtless, this humble volume notwithstanding, is soon to be subject to the hoovering of Time.

www.ingramcontent.com/pod-product-compliance
Lightning Source LLC
Chambersburg PA
CBHW020359030726
47496CB00007B/2221